A Patchwork Legacy

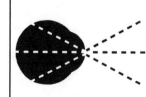

This Large Print Book carries the
Seal of Approval of N.A.V.H.

A Patchwork Legacy

ONE WOMAN'S LEGACY OF HOPE IS BESTOWED UPON TWO STRUGGLING COUPLES

RENEE DeMARCO
COLLEEN L. REECE

THORNDIKE PRESS

A part of Gale, Cengage Learning

GALE
CENGAGE Learning™

Detroit • New York • San Francisco • New Haven, Conn • Waterville, Maine • London

GALE
CENGAGE Learning™

© 2005 *Remnants of Faith* by Renee DeMarco.
© 2005 *Silver Lining* by Colleen L. Reece.
All scripture quotations are taken from the King James Version of the Bible.
Thorndike Press, a part of Gale, Cengage Learning.

Thorndike Press® Large Print Christian Fiction.
The text of this Large Print edition is unabridged.
Other aspects of the book may vary from the original edition.
Set in 16 pt. Plantin.
Printed on permanent paper.

LIBRARY OF CONGRESS CATALOGING-IN-PUBLICATION DATA

DeMarco, Renee.
    A patchwork legacy : one woman's legacy of hope is bestowed upon two struggling couples / by Renee DeMarco and Colleen L. Reece.
        p. cm. — (Thorndike Press large print Christian fiction)
    ISBN-13: 978-1-4104-1580-6 (hardcover : alk. paper)
    ISBN-10: 1-4104-1580-5 (hardcover : alk. paper)
    1. Christian fiction, American. 2. Christmas stories, American. 3. Large type books. I. DeMarco, Renee. Remnants of faith. II. Reece, Colleen L. Silver lining. III. Title.
PS648.C43D46 2009
813'.01083823—dc22   2009004543

Published in 2009 by arrangement with Colleen L. Reece.

Printed in the United States of America
1 2 3 4 5 6 7 13 12 11 10 09

■ ■ ■ ■

REMNANTS OF FAITH
BY RENEE DEMARCO

■ ■ ■ ■

DEDICATION

For Mom . . . and all those like her
who meet life's challenges
with courage, optimism, and hope.

"And Jesus said unto them . . .
If ye have faith
as a grain of mustard seed,
ye shall say unto this mountain,
Remove hence to yonder place;
and it shall remove;
and nothing shall be impossible
unto you."
MATTHEW 17:20

PROLOGUE

Boise, Idaho

The shining snow, sapphire blue sky, and dark evergreens just outside Olivia Howard Forester's apartment window were no more colorful than the pile of Christmas envelopes cluttering her quilt-draped lap. Threadbare and worn, it remained her favorite lap robe and reminded her of days long past. So many days, years, and decades! Now the world had moved into the twenty-first century. Life had been good, even though her beloved husband, Nate, had long since passed on. They had never been blessed with children of their own, but the students Olivia taught for so many years had filled the couple's lives with love.

Olivia wiped away a tear with a wrinkled hand and turned her attention to the paper remnants, printed with varied postmarks, littering the floor beside her comfortable rocking chair. Each bore witness to the far-reaching effects of her many years of teaching. She smiled and reread the scrawled personal message inside the card she had just opened.

I never forgot the advice our principal gave me when I told him I wanted to grow up and become a teacher like you, Mrs. Forester. He smiled and said, "You can do it, if you remember one thing. She isn't just in the business of teaching ABCs. She teaches children." Now, after many years in my own classroom, I understand. Thank you.

Olivia raised her head and looked out the window. The card slid to join others with similar messages that had already fallen to the carpet. What a blessing the cards were! Year after year they came, bringing joy and gladness that left her both proud and humble. "Thomas Wolfe was wrong about not being able to go home again," Olivia whispered. "These Christmas messages take me back each year."

The world outside her window faded. A wealth of memories, starting with those from her earliest recollection, gently carried her to another time.

Childish laughter mingled with the

whoosh of sleds on snow-packed streets. Older brothers and sisters pulled siblings up hills too steep for short legs. Children made snow angels. Teen boys chased girls, threatening to wash their faces with snow. Snowballs flew between hastily constructed snow forts, and snow people dotted the landscape like winter statues. Carolers swarmed through the neighborhoods, wrapped in so many layers of clothing they could barely walk, filling the night with song.

Other images formed in her mind. Christmases during a succession of world conflicts had been hard, almost unbearable, but there had always been joy. Olivia looked at her tastefully decorated Christmas tree, relieved that those times were over. Yet looking at the envelopes, she realized days of hardship were not all in the past. Despite some of her students' brave attempts to be cheerful, pain lay between the lines. Loneliness, poverty, conflict, disaster, and tragedy invaded this era as they had in days long ago. If only she could relieve some of the distress and bring comfort!

Olivia chuckled. "Foolish old woman. What little you have wouldn't lessen the suffering of ten persons, much less a hundred." Her laughter died. "Besides, many of my former students don't need money. They need love, friendship, and to know the Lord. How can I supply that?"

All that day and evening, Olivia pondered these things in her heart. She became convinced she could do something. She would select one or two individuals from among the many, but how would she know whom to choose?

"You don't have to do this alone," a small inner voice whispered. *"Remember what you learned more than half a century ago."*

"Of course!" Olivia reached for her well-used Bible and turned to James 1:5–6: " 'If any of you lack wisdom, let him ask of God, that giveth to all men liberally, and upbraideth not; and it shall be given him. But let him ask in faith, nothing wavering. For he that wavereth is like a wave of the sea driven with the wind and tossed.' "

"Thank You, Lord, for guiding me," Olivia whispered. She caught up the stack of cards and began going through them once more. The first dozen or so she discarded. Not because she didn't sense need, but because she instinctively knew they were not the right ones. The next card contained a chatty letter. Gavin Scott, the young man in whom she once delighted and despaired, had taken the time to update his former teacher on what was happening in his life. Happiness and well-being spilled from every word. Olivia laughed when she read the postscript:

"I've been so busy, I haven't had time to find a woman with whom to share my life. God willing, someday I will."

She tossed the card down with the others. Obviously, all was well with him. He had no need of her inheritance.

The next to the last card offered no news, no hint of what was going on in the sender's life, only a one-word signature, "Natalie," written in the distinctive script Olivia immediately recognized. Interesting. Her former student must not be married or she would have signed her full name.

Gavin's words, "too busy . . . a woman to share my life . . . God willing . . ." beat into Olivia's brain, followed by a daring idea. The two writers were within a few years of each other in age but not close enough to have overlapped in school. What if their teacher were to make it possible for Gavin and Natalie to meet?

Olivia chuckled. "At this moment a matchmaker is born!" The more she thought and prayed about it, the more she was convinced it might be God's will for her to carry out

13

her plans. First, she would sleep on it. She placed the small stack of cards on her night-stand. "I need Your confirmation, Lord. Please help me know if this is who You want me to choose." Within minutes, sleep claimed her.

More snow fell on Boise during the long night hours. A white cape blanketed the city. Fence posts and mailboxes donned jaunty ermine caps. When Olivia awakened, she sat bolt upright in bed and snatched up the cards over which she had earnestly prayed. Her fingers shook with excitement. The warm glow in her heart confirmed God's approval. Gavin and Natalie were the right two.

After breakfast, Olivia called a lawyer friend. "I want to make a new will. Can you come today?"

"Of course, if you feel it's urgent. Are you ill?" Mr. Graves asked.

"No. I'd just like to get my affairs in order before the holiday rush."

"I'll drop over around two," he promised.

Olivia cradled the phone and smiled.

Long before her attorney arrived, Olivia knew exactly what she wanted in her will. The two people named would need to understand and abide by her wishes and conditions.

If Mr. Graves thought the will odd, only an amused twitch of his lips now and then betrayed him. At one point in the discussion he chuckled. "Up to your old tricks, are you? You always did have a way of getting people to do what you wanted! But love has a mind of its own."

"Sometimes it can use a little shove," she retorted. "How soon can you get copies made?"

"You are in a rush," he teased. "No problem. I'll have them prepared and bring them back for you to sign this evening." He rose. "You're up to something, Olivia Forester. I can always tell." He was still smiling when he went out. A few hours later, the new will was properly signed and witnessed. Mr. Graves wished Olivia a happy Christmas and rose to leave.

"Thank you," she replied. "I have a feeling this is going to be my best Christmas ever."

"I wouldn't be a bit surprised," her attorney agreed.

When he had gone, Olivia plugged in the lights on her Christmas tree. She thought about the man and woman she had chosen to list in her new will. Suddenly they seemed more important than all the students she had ever taught. Would her crazy scheme to help them work?

Just before midnight on Christmas Eve, Olivia Forester sat in her comfortable rocking chair. Her worn hands lay in her quilt-clad lap, clasping two cards. The clear, steady glow from the Bethlehem star on top of her Christmas tree filled Olivia's heart with longing. "Father," she said, "more than two thousand years ago, wise men traveled a long, hard road. They followed the star until they found the Master. I've done all I can to help my chosen students on their journeys. The rest is up to You."

The mantel clock struck twelve, ushering in another Christmas and bringing peace to Olivia Forester's giving heart.

CHAPTER 1

Washington State, the following November

The door slammed shut, but not before the icy fingers of a Seattle November evening reached in and put a physical exclamation point on Mark Thorsett's bitter words that still lingered in the air.

"I'm finished. I can't do this any longer."

Through the night, Natalie, his petite, brunette wife, replayed the evening's events through sleep-deprived, teary eyes. How could it have gotten this bad? Only the soft breaths of her sleeping seven- and five-year-old daughters answered. Mark and her relationship hadn't always been marked by the turmoil of late. She remembered fondly the days when friends and strangers would freely approach them and ask the secret of their obviously strong relationship.

Mark would look at her with his ocean blue eyes, wink, and jest, "No secret at all. Anyone married to Natalie would have it easy."

He'd place his arms, strong from physical labor, protectively around her, and she'd melt back into his embrace. Had someone told her back during those blissful post-honeymoon days that she'd ever have cause to question the foundation of their relationship, she would have laughed them out of the room. Natalie wasn't laughing now.

Mark's frosty farewell, though reminiscent of conversations of late, held a finality she hadn't heard before. *Would he really leave the kids and me?* The question taunted her weary mind into the predawn hours. Her writhing gut played counterpoint to her mind's adamant *no.*

The fact that she, Natalie Thorsett, poster child for mother and wife of the year, was even asking the question spoke volumes of the tumultuous past couple of years. Glancing around the barren shell of the one-room space they now called home put an exclamation point on the experience. To say life had dealt them a series of unfortunate blows was to put it lightly. A flagging economy and poor annual sales figures in his engineering firm had left Mark with a pink slip in hand. He had enough time under his belt to hold on through the first round of layoffs, but his lack of age and experience sank him in the second round. While others facing the same fate had panicked, Natalie and Mark had unified in faith, sure that another, better opportunity lay just around the corner. Neither had the slightest inkling that the corner would be over two years away. Or how incredibly treacherous those two years would be.

Natalie shivered, partly from the memories, but more from the chill of the room that evidenced poor workmanship and lack of insulation. Oh, what she would give to be soaking in the tub she had once deemed too small in her suburban dream home. The glut of unemployed Northwest engineers and lack of jobs had turned the Thorsetts' job search from days into weeks. When those weeks turned into years, they had been forced to sell their possessions to make ends meet.

First it was the extras. The entertainment center. A newly purchased ivory and muted rose sofa and love seat set. The bedroom furniture they had given each other as a wedding gift.

Then it was cashing out their retirement accounts. Taking out credit cards. Avoiding bill collectors. Natalie had picked up part-time work where she could to help out, but her lack of a college education had relegated her to a series of minimum-wage fast-food jobs. Through it all, Mark bolstered the family with faith-based scriptures and his positive attitude.

"When life gives you lemons . . ." became Mark's mantra. It was always followed by a shouted youthful duet of "the Thorsetts make lemonade!" The girls would propel themselves across floors and over couches into Mark's waiting arms. The giggle festival that invariably followed brought a smile to Natalie's face then — and now.

The bittersweet memories rubbed raw on the night's open wounds. Banishing them from her mind, she rose from the side of the threadbare twin bed she and Mark shared to check on her sleeping girls.

Even in restless slumber, the innocence of youth permeated the area where they clung together. Seven-year-old Amber had her arm protectively around her little sister Mollie's small frame. Amber's bravery through the last couple of years brought tears to Natalie's eyes. No matter what life served up, Amber met it with optimism. With both parents trying to make the finances work, Amber had stepped into the role of part-time mother for her younger sister. The faith of a child.

"How will that faith hold up if Mark really leaves?" Natalie's words lingered unnaturally in the frigid room.

As much as she wanted to deny the possibility, Natalie couldn't. The Mark of late bore little resemblance to the leader who once guided and directed their home. The loss of their house and the journey into a series of increasingly more squalid dwellings had been one lemon Mark Thorsett couldn't convert into a pleasant drink. Natalie had seen the progressive toll guilt had waged on his soul. His inability to provide for his family had eaten away at his self-esteem and left a crust of a man. While some of their acquaintances in similar circumstances had sought refuge in controlled substances, Mark had refused that method of escape. Instead, his personal path had led to depression and anger.

"Anger that caused him to make rash statements he didn't mean," Natalie whispered, remembering his parting words earlier.

"Oh, Lord, please let them be statements he didn't mean." At the sound of her own prayerful words, Natalie Thorsett came face-to-face with the reality of the present. Her husband, the love of her life, the father of her children, might not be coming back.

Natalie fell to the cold floor, clutching her grieving heart in indescribable pain.

Through broken sobs she cried, "Father, I can't do this. I'm not strong enough. I don't want to be a single mom. I don't want my husband to leave. Please make this go away. Let me come stay with You for a little while where I don't have to feel this."

Her cries softened to quiet whispers. "I love him, Lord. Please bring him back. My girls and I need him." She paused and added, "And, Lord, my girls and I really need You."

After many long hours, sleep finally released Natalie Thorsett from the anguish of the night's events. In the throes of slumber the icy floor numbed her limbs and body, even as a warm heavenly embrace surrounded her heart.

CHAPTER 2

If someone had told Natalie Thorsett she would ever feel more discouraged than she had on the November night a month ago when Mark left, she would have called them crazy. Yet here she was, on December 10, facing the bleakest holiday she could ever remember. Mark, true to his word, had left. A couple of letters had come since, but amidst the greetings to the girls and the attempt to put an optimistic spin on his fruitless job search, were layers of pain. The postmarks told a story of travel down the I-5 corridor south, but the last letter had come with a Portland, Oregon, postmark.

"He's left the state," Natalie whispered, turning the envelope over in her shaking hands.

Hope that the letter might also contain some much-needed cash or news of a new job fled as she opened the envelope and a single sheet of paper floated to the floor. Usually he had managed to send a few dollars here and there from part-time work, which, coupled with Natalie's meager earnings, had managed to keep her head just above the water.

With Christmas just days away, things had never been worse financially.

Resigned to what she had to do, Natalie fought back her pride and sat down to write the letter she should have sent weeks ago. She carefully addressed her letter to the scrawled return address in Portland, Oregon, and then began.

Dear Mark,

I'm sorry about our fight. I said some things I never should have said. It's just that it's been so hard to recognize you lately. I can't tell you how much I miss the man I married, the man who has carried us through the tough times with humor and optimism. I know you feel that our financial woes are somehow your fault, but they aren't. Life isn't always easy. We were never promised it would be. I don't blame you — I wish you wouldn't blame yourself. You have done your best. I just miss having you around — the real you. The girls need you, too. We could live in a tent, but if we were together as a family, that would be enough for me.

I don't know how much longer I can make the money stretch. We are already behind on rent, but I think the landlord will give us an extension — I just don't know how much time he will give us. They turned the telephone service off yesterday, so if you decide to call, it won't go through. I'm scared, Mark. I really wish you were here. I pray for you every day. Whether or not you find a job, if you decide you want us to come — we will be there in a heartbeat. I love you and believe in you. Please forgive me. I really want to work this out. If you want to give us another chance, as well, please let me know.

All my love,
Natalie

Natalie slowly licked the envelope and walked down the street to the public mailbox. Pausing before depositing the letter, she whispered a prayer. "Please help this find my husband, and please wrap Your arms around him as he reads it. He needs not only my love but Yours. Give us a new start."

25

Ten days later the mail provided an unwelcome answer. Two envelopes arrived. The one she had sent Mark days earlier had been stamped "Addressee Unknown." Mark would not be coming home. The second came with a postmark from Idaho.

"I don't know anyone in Idaho," Natalie muttered. "I wonder if Mark has gone all the way up there?"

Opening the envelope provided a definitive no to her second question. The letter, on official-looking paper, was from a legal office: Graves and Billings, Professional Corporation.

She scanned the enclosed text with interest.

We regret to inform you of the passing of Mrs. Olivia Howard Forester. You have been identified as a conditional beneficiary under the terms of her last will and testament. She has indicated that you are to receive a designated item of personal property under the conditions and terms set forth in the will. We have enclosed, for your signature, a release. Upon receipt of your signed release, we shall tender the bequest to you per the terms of her testamentary document. If you have any questions or comments, please do not hesitate to call.

Sincerely,

Bill Graves, Attorney-at-Law

Natalie's emotions raced. Olivia Forester, her beloved teacher, dead? But a bequest! "What could it be? Maybe the money we desperately need to pay the rent? Or will it be something of value that I can sell or pawn to pay bills?"

Natalie put down the letter and headed for the door. The young couple in the apartment across from them had been very good about letting her use their phone since Natalie no longer had phone service of her own. The lawyer had left a toll-free number where he could be contacted.

Once inside the walls of her neighbor's comparatively warm house, Natalie dialed the number, shaking with anticipation. Could this be the Lord's answer to her mounting financial woes?

"Law offices of Graves and Billings, may I help you?" the official-sounding voice queried.

"Um, I'm Natalie Thorsett and I received a letter about being left something in the will of Mrs. Forester."

"One moment. I'll transfer you to Mr. Graves."

A deep, warm older voice resonated from the line. "Ms. Thorsett? How are you? I assume you are calling about Olivia's will."

"Yes, I am." Natalie's voice trembled. "What was I left, if you don't mind my asking?"

"Not at all, dear." Mr. Graves chuckled. "You know that Olivia; she always did things a little outside of the box. She left you what she deemed her most prized possession — her heirloom quilt. But there is a condition. At the end of one year, you must deliver it to another individual whom she has named. She has provided in the will the financial arrangements for you to take such a journey to deliver the quilt."

Mr. Graves's words rolled off Natalie like water off a rock. After the word "quilt," she found herself unable to hear much else, awash in a sea of dashed hopes.

"Anything you ask," she managed to force out. "I'll send you the release. Thank you."

It was only later, in her home, after Amber and Mollie were tucked securely into the twin bed she and Mark once shared, that Natalie allowed herself to think of the day's events.

"Mrs. Forester . . . gone?" Even speaking the words didn't make them any more believable.

Mrs. Forester had been Natalie's safe place when, during her third-grade year, Natalie's own mom had succumbed to cancer. Olivia had seen through the shy girl's rapidly constructed facade and had invited her into the home she and her husband, Nate, infused with warmth. Never having grandparents of her own, Natalie was informally adopted by Olivia and Nate Forester, grandparents-in-training. They had embraced the little girl with love and friendship. After school each night, she had been invited into the Foresters' home until her dad could pick her up after he got off work. Those afternoon hours had been among the best of Natalie's life. Baking cookies, learning to knit, sitting and reading stories with Olivia, fishing and whittling with Nate. Natalie's days had been filled beyond measure.

Remembering the sweet days of the past infused Natalie with a warm longing. The Foresters' home had been such a sweet refuge from her childhood storms, much like Mark's arms had been for many years of her adult life. Now, when she needed it the most, neither harbor was available to her. Shaking off the thought that threatened to plunge her into a well of pity, Natalie once again looked over the letter from the attorney's office.

"Why would Olivia leave me a quilt? Why would the quilt be her most prized possession? And who is this person I'm supposed to be giving it to?"

Knowing none of the questions could be answered without the passage of considerable time, Natalie shivered up to the children in the bed thats only warmth came from the three huddled bodies beneath its thin cover.

"Well, my inheritance may not be money, but right now a warm blanket would be a real blessing. I hope it comes quickly." Tired beyond measure, Natalie punctuated the last sentiment with a soft snore.

CHAPTER 3

Natalie Thorsett closed her eyes and willed a few extra moments in the blissful dream world she had been so abruptly thrust from. So clear were her imaginings, she could almost touch the dark-haired, blue-eyed, smiling Mark. It had been the Christmas morning after they were married. Memories mingled with the sweet leftovers from her dreams. Neither she nor Mark had experienced the joy of firmly established Christmas traditions when they were children. Her father had found Christmas memories without his beloved wife too painful, and Mark's parents had figured that their once-yearly Christmas Eve trek to church was more than enough tradition for them.

Not Mark or Natalie. They had vowed early in their relationship to instill sweet, warm traditions throughout the Christmas holidays. Celebrating Christ's birth in the

Thorsett family was going to be something special.

It had started the year they were married. Mark had awakened her at 12:01 a.m. Christmas Day.

"Talie," Mark began tenderly, using the special name only he used. "Time to get up. It's our first Thorsett Christmas."

Natalie, never one for early mornings — especially not this early — had groggily protested, until the smell of fresh bacon had serenaded her senses. She shuffled the short distance between their apartment bedroom and kitchen. There, a full-fledged breakfast extravaganza greeted her. Not only had Mark prepared bacon, it was bent to look like candy canes. The pancakes were slightly misshapen snowmen, the fruit cut into Christmas trees, and the eggs molded into ornaments.

"What is this?" Natalie asked, unsuccessfully hiding her bemused smile.

Mark's ear-to-ear grin had said it all. "You said you wanted Christmas tradition, Mrs. Natalie Thorsett. You got it."

Mark had been true to his word. The Thorsetts did Christmas like no other family Natalie knew. Amidst all the fun, though, her favorite tradition had not changed. At that first midnight breakfast, Mark had pulled out his Bible and began to read.

" 'And it came to pass in those days, that there went out a decree from Caesar Augustus, that all the world should be taxed.' " In his gentle, emotion-tinged voice, Mark read the Christmas story.

Once again, before retiring to bed, Mark had gathered with Natalie and read from the Bible the passages concerning Christ's birth. Even as some of the holiday traditions had been replaced with others as the girls got older, each year Mark had continued to insist that the day start, and end, the way it should — remembering the Savior's birth. Not a present was touched, not a morsel eaten, until Dad, often flannel-pajama-clad, welcomed the day with the heralding words of the angels: " 'Glory to God in the highest, and on earth peace, good will toward men.' "

Like Natalie, the girls came to love this tradition more than any other. This year, while it appeared most of their traditions would have to be put on hold, the girls had only asked about one. Their recent questions had revolved around how Dad would read them the Christmas story this year. Natalie had attempted to sidestep the questions, not sure of the answers herself.

Thoughts of unanswered questions propelled Natalie unwillingly to the present. Getting out of bed and gathering a thin blanket around her, she dejectedly slumped against the barren, drafty wall. Her gaze fell on the tilting branch in the corner, trying to pass itself off as a Christmas tree. Who ever heard of decorating a pine limb? When informed there would be no tree this year, Amber and Mollie had dragged the downed branch from a local ditch, stood it upright in a plastic bucket half full of rocks, and christened it "The Thorsett Family Tree." The hanging snowflakes, cut from old newspapers collected along the road, didn't help the image.

Glancing across the room at her two sleeping children huddled together in thin blankets, Natalie's frustration mounted. *They sleep on an old mattress. They eat whatever meager rations I can scrounge for them. It's been over a year since I could even buy them a new pair of shoes. Haven't we all been through enough?*

Natalie looked at the two presents beneath the tree. She shuddered, thinking how disappointed the children would be to find two-liter soda bottles under the newspaper wrapping. Probably not as disappointed as finding out there wouldn't be Mark's traditional Christmas turkey. Somehow, she didn't think boxed macaroni and cheese would get the same reception. Natalie's biggest concern, though, had nothing to do with the food or the gifts. How would the girls get through Christmas without the man who was the center of their existence? Needless to say, it would be a far cry from Christmases past — Christmases when Mark was with them.

Natalie's musings were interrupted by Amber's quiet voice. "Mom, are you thinking about Dad?"

Natalie looked at the mussed dark brown hair of her oldest child. "Yes, honey, I am."

"It's okay, Mom. I miss him, too." Amber's eyes contained a knowing look befitting one far older than she. "I sure hope he can make it home. We have each other. He doesn't have anyone. Who will he read the Christmas story to?"

Natalie had to turn away so Amber wouldn't see the tears her daughter's selflessness had triggered. *Here I've been thinking only about the girls and myself and how awful this Christmas will be. How lonely it will be for Mark.*

At her silence, Amber continued. "You know what I think we should do? We should draw him pictures and write him stories of all our favorite Christmas memories. That way, he can tape them on his wall and look around all Christmas Day and feel like he's doing all the things with us."

Natalie rose and put her arms around Amber. "That's a wonderful idea. I'm not sure how we will get them to him, but we'll try."

"Mom, he'll get them." Assurance resonated from Amber's voice. "You are the one who tells us that all things are possible through Christ."

"Yes, honey, you're right." Even as Natalie said the words, she wasn't sure exactly how much she believed them right now.

If she had cause to question the scripture when Amber quoted it, her questions only increased as the day went on.

December 21 was not a red-letter day for Natalie Thorsett. It was, however, a red-notice day. A THREE-DAY NOTICE TO PAY RENT OR VACATE day. Natalie stared at the piece of red paper taped hastily to their door. Handwritten on the bottom of the note was a scribbled, "I'll give you till December 26 as a Christmas present."

"The creep." Even with the pit of terror in her stomach growing, Natalie still felt anger at the spiteful, unfriendly old man who deemed evicting a family on the day after

Christmas instead of Christmas Day his charitable deed for the year. She crumpled the notice into her pocket, determined that her girls would not learn this news until after they had celebrated Christmas.

Once within the walls of the apartment, which suddenly looked pretty good, Natalie fell to her knees in prayer. "Dear heavenly Father, please help us. I don't know what to do. I'm scared. I used to think I could do anything through You, but I'm just not sure anymore. Please strengthen my feeble knees. If it were only me affected by this, I'd be okay, but my daughters are just little girls. They belong in nice warm beds, not living on the streets. You love little children. I know You do. Please protect mine. In Jesus' name, amen."

Natalie's hope that a last-minute reprieve might come through a large sum of cash in the mail or a knock on her door telling her she'd won a sweepstakes did not play out. The mail, however, did bring two items that sent the girls into a frenzy of excitement.

"Two packages, Mom." Mollie's freckles stood out on her pale cheeks like stars in the winter night sky. "What could they be?"

Knowing the next few days would not hold much happiness for her dear children, Natalie wanted to prolong these moments.

"I don't know. Why don't you open them?"

"Can we really, Mom? You are the best." The unison response brought a slight smile to Natalie's troubled countenance.

The girls ripped into the packages with the wild abandon of Christmases long past. The first bore a letter, which Amber opened and began to read.

Dear Family,

My job search has not been as successful as I hoped. Since I won't be with you this year, I wanted to send you my Bible.

Amber, I have marked the special passages that I read each year. If you will wake everyone up one minute after midnight and read the marked verses, I will wake up here at that time and think about you reading them.

I know this Christmas isn't the way any of us wanted it to be. Certainly not me. Just remember — Christmas is not about us. It's about Jesus.

I love you girls. Merry Christmas.

Dad

As the girls turned to the other package, Natalie carefully cradled the worn Bible that stirred so many memories of better days and years. Would she ever again know the joy of those long-lost times? The gleeful voices of her girls caused her to focus on the other package. Amber and Mollie were in the process of lifting a quilt out of a box. As they gave one final tug, the folds dwarfed the two of them as they collapsed on the floor. Looking at her girls wrapped like Christmas packages, Natalie was caught by the beauty of the old handcrafted master-piece. In the dismal, undecorated apart-ment, its still-vivid colors seemed alive with light.

"Oh, Mom. It's the warmest, softest blanket I've ever felt. And it's big enough for all of us — even Dad. Isn't it the bestest present you've ever seen? God must have told someone we needed a warm blanket." Mollie, the more reserved of her daughters, gushed with enthusiasm.

Mollie's exuberance was catching. Natalie burst into laughter and joined the girls in the embrace of the woolen remnants stitched with love. She knew the piece of paper in the bottom of the paper carton must shed light on the origin of the price-less possession, but she set the paper aside for another day. She was going to capture the joy of this moment. Snuggled beneath the generous cover with her precious daugh-ters, Natalie allowed herself to dream of better times to come. In the arms of the quilt, she quietly hoped. She touched each lovingly stitched square as the girls glued their little bodies to her. Fabric swatches, which individually bespoke little glory, blended together into a magnificent creation. The person who had created it must have had vision.

Like my little seeds of faith, Natalie thought. *Not much on their own, but perhaps together they'll make something beautiful.*

Glancing back down at the heirloom quilt, Natalie whispered, "Remnants of faith. Perhaps Olivia has sent us remnants of faith."

CHAPTER 4

If Mark Thorsett believed life would get better when he walked out of his Seattle apartment a few weeks ago, he had another think coming. As miserable as being jobless, depressed, angry, and poor was, it wasn't as bad as being jobless, depressed, angry, poor, *and* lonely. His last exchange with Natalie sent him into fits of guilt during those rare moments he was able to pull himself out of his self-pitying reverie, to boot.

He was having one of those treasured "kick me in the stomach" moments now. Watching mothers and children shop for the Christmas holidays in downtown Eugene, Oregon, conjured up thoughts of his girls at home. Boy, he really missed them. Ever since he and Natalie married, Christmas had been the pinnacle of his year.

Feeling the sudden chill of the winter wind, Mark bundled his threadbare coat around his bonier-than-usual shoulders and

41

muttered, "Christmas certainly won't be the highlight of this year."

He had sent his well-worn Bible home to Amber so that she could read the Christmas story. Their Christmas would be better without him home anyway.

After moving progressively southward in search of work, he had just secured a temporary part-time construction job in Eugene. Of course, December was not the busiest of construction times in the Northwest, but he was making more than the Golden Arches had offered. At this point he would have dredged sewers to garnish enough coins to provide himself lodging and send some home. Turning the corner from his new employer's office, Mark was heralded by the familiar ringing of bells. Natalie was always giving to the bell ringers. Mark couldn't recollect a time she had passed one by, even in the poorest times, without depositing some offering.

"Well, Talie," Mark whispered, searching his pockets for orphan change, "this is for you."

His meager deposit sounded puny as it joined few other coins in the holly berry red Salvation Army can.

"God bless." The ringer's soft-spoken voice was a perfect match for his snow-white hair and gently worn face.

"I sure wish He would." Mark's spoken response surprised even him.

The edges of the man's blue eyes wrinkled at the corners. Placing his hand on Mark's arm, he spoke. "Son, I believe He has sent you plenty of blessings. You just have to open your eyes to see them."

Mark stammered a few socially polite responses and then uncomfortably hurried on his way. The last thing he needed was advice from a stranger.

What does he know? How can he say I've been blessed? I've lost everything. I lost my job. I have no money. I can't support my family financially, and now, when they need me the most, I'm not there. I have no friends. I'm a terrible husband and father. I'm sleeping on a flea-infested mattress in an old building with a bunch of strangers in a town I've never set foot in before. I may be a lot of things, but blessed is not one of them. Mark's thoughts became a bitter avalanche as he angrily strode down the concrete sidewalks to the shelter where he was bedding down on a cot.

"I loved God. I served Him. I don't know what I've done to anger Him, but it must have been something terrible. I haven't seen a blessing in months. Maybe even years!"

With that, Mark ran a hand through his dark, curly hair and stamped his foot with a finality that would have convinced even the most apathetic onlooker, had there been one.

Late into the night Mark's words floated through the land between sleep and awake. Visions of his girls. Midnight Christmas breakfasts. Natalie running on the beach. After hours of restless slumber, Mark Thorsett had to admit he once had been incredibly blessed. He longed for those days — the days when he had found favor with God and men. But, as in his dreams, they were too far away to reach.

The days leading up to Christmas were almost unbearable for the man who had become the guru of Christmas traditions. On his hours off, he took to walking the Willamette River. Swollen from heavy rain, the waters took on an almost brown cast. Beside the rushing torrent, he could almost forget the memories. Almost.

"If I hadn't been so good at creating them, I wouldn't have so many memories tormenting me right now," Mark wryly admitted to himself.

Slouching down on a bench, Mark stared at the angry river. Suddenly, a slightly familiar voice made him look up.

"Mind if I join you?"

Mark's ocean blue gaze met that of the Salvation Army bell ringer.

"Jack Pace." The man's smile seemed to stretch all the way down to his hand, which he extended for a shake.

Mark obliged. "I'm Mark Thorsett."

"Well, Mark, I must say I've seen a lot of heartbreak this holiday season. You know, ringing bells all day, you get a chance to watch people very closely. You see the arguers and the criers. The exhausted mothers and the fathers who want very much to be anywhere else. You see the lonely. You see those who have lost companions and those who are longing for them. You see those who are remembering the real reason for the Christmas celebration and those who don't have a clue what it is all about."

Jack paused and then looked up at Mark. "But you know, son, of all the folks I've seen this year, I haven't seen one as lost or as sad as you. Don't suppose you want to talk about it?"

Mark looked at the kindness emanating from the older gentleman's well-lined face and suddenly felt as though he did want to talk. As he opened up, years of pent-up frustration, depression, self-doubt, and pain poured out like the torrential Willamette, whose clamorous flow kept his story company.

After a steady hour, Mark was spent. He slumped against the weathered bench, waiting for the disgust, condemnation, and judgment he was sure were coming from this obviously good man. To his surprise, Jack remained peacefully silent.

When he finally did open his mouth, it was not to condemn. "I can see why you are so sad, my boy. I can tell you love your wife and children very much, maybe as much as I loved my Marjorie. It's nearly five years she's been gone, but I still wake up every day expecting to see her gentle face next to mine. Every minute I lived with that woman was joyous. Memories of those wonderful moments are blessings that keep me company every day until my Lord sees fit that I join her." Jack's lip quivered. Regaining his composure, he continued.

"Son, we lived through the Depression. There were times we didn't know where the next meal would come from. Sometimes it didn't come. I'd stand in long lines waiting for a chance to work for one day at a place. We didn't know how, but we knew that even without food or shelter, God would provide. They were happy times because we had each other.

"We lived through the war. Separated. Never knowing which letter would be the last. But they, too, were happy days because we knew our love would last beyond this life, and each moment became precious.

"I'm sure we had some of the same issues that face all couples today, but I vowed when I married her that I would do as much for my sweet companion as I could." Jack paused and placed his arm on Mark's shoulder.

"Selflessness, repentance, and inviting your heavenly Father into your life on a daily basis. The Key Three, I like to call them."

Mark looked at the old man. "Do you think there is still hope for me? For us?"

Jack winked and then rose to leave. "Do you think I'd be sitting here if I didn't? Let your wife know you still love her. Then come see me tomorrow. I'll be ringing on my street corner, and we'll start the process of taking care of you."

Walking back to the shelter, Mark felt a small ray of hope pierce his bitter and wounded heart.

"Selflessness, repentance, and You." Inwardly measuring his standing in each category, Mark shook his head. "Well, I guess everyone has to start building somewhere. Even if it is ground zero."

With his declaration of intent, Mark Thorsett took out a pen and began to write the letter he had wanted to write for a long time. A letter claiming responsibility — and telling Natalie how much she was loved. Most of all, it would be a letter expressing his remorse. It was a letter long in the works, but if Jack Pace were right — and Mark sure hoped he was — Mark had just taken the first step along a road to healing.

CHAPTER 5

"Homeless." The word sounded as foreign and strange as Natalie Thorsett felt. This was the stuff of other people's nightmares, not hers.

"Funny, I feel the same as I did yesterday, when I had a place to come home to," Natalie mused. "Yet nothing is the same."

January 2 was not one of the Thorsetts' better days. Natalie was grateful the girls were back in school; Amber was doing well in second grade, and Mollie loved her all-day kindergarten class. Natalie hadn't yet found the courage or words to inform the principal of their plight. In fact, she was still debating whether she would have to. "As long as I have them to the bus stop every morning, no one will be the wiser." Even as she said the words, however, she knew they didn't ring true.

Natalie needed help. This was one secret that needed as many people working on it as possible. She had managed to secure the next two weeks at a local women and children's shelter, but the head of the facility had been clear: Winter was busy. Too busy. Demand outstripped supply by leaps and bounds. Each bed had a waiting list with multiple names. People were waiting, hoping for a night's sleep away from damp freeway underpasses and makeshift tarps.

Gingerly making her way down the pavement layered with ice, Natalie clutched her jacket around her shoulders. Shopkeepers were diligently removing seasonal decorations and boxing them up for storage. Post-Christmas return-laden shoppers brushed by her, hurrying to take care of unfinished business.

Natalie and the girls wouldn't be returning any packages this year. Other than the two brightly wrapped bottles of sparkly soda, there hadn't been any presents under the Thorsett limb. Despite the obvious contrasts with Christmases past, the girls had dutifully followed Mark's directive, rising at midnight to read the story of Christ's birth. Somehow this year, the young Mary and Joseph trying to find shelter when the inn was full struck a painfully familiar chord with Natalie. There had been no room for them anywhere, either.

Natalie had known only too well, when she had hurriedly tucked the THREE-DAY NOTICE TO PAY RENT OR VACATE into a drawer, that it foreshadowed a not-too-far-distant time when she also would be searching for a place for her sweet family to lay down and rest.

Now the time was upon her. Natalie shook her head. With the gesture, the memories from last week fled like the foraging pigeons she startled. There had been no further word from Mark, even after her plea for help and forgiveness. Natalie reconciled herself to the idea that he must have decided to move on. Sadness gripped her heart more piercingly than the bitter cold. She banished the feelings. Right now she couldn't afford to think of anything but getting food on her girls' plates and a place for them to have refuge from the cold.

She plopped down onto a well-used bench, relieved to find rest from lugging around the bag that almost equaled her in size. The process of deciding what to take had been more difficult than she expected, given how little they had. Clothes and blankets took up the lion's share of the space. A few precious keepsakes, including Mark's Bible, had filled the remaining space. Looking out over Puget Sound, Natalie lifted the largest quilt from the bag. Olivia Forester's quilt. As she opened its folds, an envelope fell to the ground. Funny, she hadn't seen it since the day the quilt had arrived. Her icy fingers fumbled to manipulate the paper. Once opened, a familiar handwritten script greeted Natalie.

My dearest Natalie,

I am sitting here, rocking in my chair, remembering a time when we used to sit together and read stories. When you get to be my age, memories become your best friends. You have given me plenty of fond ones. For some reason I feel compelled to send you this quilt and to tell you the story of where it came from.

When I was a young woman, a raging fire just before Christmas took my ancestral home and everything I owned, except for the family Bible. Insurance replaced my material things, but I really struggled. Not long after that, a reporter did an article on my loss. Soon afterward, a large package arrived. A Pennsylvania family named Fisher had read the article. They felt God wanted them to send me the patchwork quilt the first Mrs. Fisher had made during her last days on earth. It was a reminder to her husband of her love — and God's. Every time I touched the beautiful covering, it helped bring comfort and healing. I feel sometimes as if God's own arms wrap around me in its folds.

I am nearing the end of my earthly journey. I look forward to meeting the Master Quilter. May my most priceless earthly possession be a reminder: God uses the tattered bits and pieces of our lives to create something beautiful and lasting.

I am not sure how this quilt will touch your life, but I can promise you this: It will.

With love,
Olivia Forester

Natalie wiped the tears that rolled down her cheeks and pressed the letter to her breast. Memories of times spent with Olivia infused the letter with warmth. Natalie wasn't sure how the quilt would make a difference in her life, but she knew that even in the short time since its arrival, the generous folds had warmed and healed and comforted her small family. *Even now,* she thought, *though its fabric is not nearly thick enough to stave off today's frigid temperatures, I feel no chill.*

After gazing out across the white-capped waves tossed by the whim of the bitter wind, Natalie rose to her feet. Tucking the quilt and letter securely back in the bag that literally held all of her earthly possessions, Natalie hefted the heavy load onto her thin shoulders and turned to leave.

"Excuse me, lovely lady." The thin masculine voice sent an unexplainable chill down Natalie's spine. She turned to face its owner.

A gentleman overdressed in leather and fur finery leered down at her. His jet-black hair sharply set off an unnaturally pale face. Despite the fact that he was obviously approaching middle age, his face showed no lines. It was as if an eraser had removed any trace of emotion or experience from the man's countenance.

Natalie was grateful her coat covered the back of her neck, where each hair stood at attention. "May I help you?" she mustered, surprised her voice was much more assertive than she felt.

"I noticed you sitting over here all by your lonesome, and I am always on the lookout for a damsel in distress." His beady eyes surveyed her like an X ray. "Especially a fine-looking one. Now, why don't you let ol' Kinsey help you."

The silky smooth voice wrapped its way

around Natalie's confidence the way a boa constrictor encircles its prey before the final, deadly squeeze. She stretched herself to her full five-feet-two-inch height, hoping the layers of clothing might make her seem more substantial. "I'm not in distress, and the last person I need help from is you. Good day, Mr. Kinsey — or should I say have a good life, since I am sure we will not meet again."

Kinsey looked at the bag slung over Natalie's shoulder, and with a chuckle that raised goose bumps that Natalie didn't even know she had, he responded, "Oh, my little beauty, to the contrary. I'm sure we will meet again." He bowed stiffly at the waist, and with a lift of his leather beret, he turned and headed down the street, serenading himself with strains of "Some Enchanted Evening."

Natalie shook her fingers, hoping to restore the blood that had drained from them. Adrenaline pumping, she half-walked, half-ran in the opposite direction the man had strolled. Natalie had always taught her children not to judge others, but for the first time in her life, she was trashing her own advice. She didn't need any further conversation to determine that this man was one she truly never wanted to see again. The evil aura around him rivaled nothing she had previously encountered.

She worriedly glanced backward a dozen times on the way to pick her children up at the bus stop. She did not want to be followed. After quickly hugging the girls, she set off with them for the shelter. Darkness set in and cast an ominous air over the Seattle streets. Natalie drew the girls closer as she passed each alleyway. She tried to stay close to the well-dressed masses leaving workplaces to head home.

After blocks of walking, Natalie spotted the shelter. The brick walls of the building welcomed the small family from the icy cold that was not generated solely by the weather. Heat poured into the street when Natalie opened the door to the entryway.

Before the girls could set their belongings down, huge black arms surrounded them. "Oh, let's get these babies in out of that cold. Get them some blankets and warm chocolate."

For the next five minutes, the Thorsett clan stood speechless as they were wrapped, warmed, and otherwise cared for by a dozen hands. Only after they were secure in front of a raging fireplace were introductions made.

"I am LouEllen." The two-hundred-plus-pound African American woman extended one of the large hands that had initially encircled the family. "I'm what they call the boss around here."

She looked down at the two wide-eyed girls and plopped down between them. Arms encircling their shoulders, she continued, "You two babies. You can call me Mama El. That's what I let my favorites call me. Now, you two want to help me with supper while your mama gets your stuff upstairs?"

Natalie watched in amazement as her two smiling girls clamored behind Mama El into the kitchen. She took her bag up to two empty cots that had been reserved for the girls and her. She pushed the cots together and then fished in the bag for the quilt. It covered both beds welcomingly. Glancing out the window before heading downstairs, she caught the shadow of a man gazing at the shelter. Fear gripped her as she recognized the leather cap adorning his head. She drew the curtain and moved quickly from the window. Grabbing the quilt off the bed, she wrapped it securely around her and closed her eyes. In a few moments, the welcoming spirit of the shelter and the folds of the blanket had worked its wonder. Peace filled Natalie's soul. It was, as Olivia Forester had put it, like the arms of God Himself had wrapped themselves around her. Natalie knelt and offered thanks. She knew that no matter what evil lurked outside, tonight she and her girls were safe in the watchful care of their heavenly Father.

CHAPTER 6

Mark Thorsett stared at the envelope in his clenched hand and tried to stem the mounting frustration that threatened to overflow. The red-stamped words, "Addressee Unknown. Return to Sender," taunted him. For the third time in as many weeks, Mark's letter to Natalie and the girls had been returned. His numerous daily phone calls had been equally unsuccessful. The operator's monotonous recorded message, "I'm sorry. The number you are trying to reach is no longer in service," kept him company throughout each waking hour.

"Where is my family?" The question hung unnaturally in the gray Eugene fog.

Calls to the landlord had gone unreturned. Mark knew his family was in desperate need of the money he was trying to send. He also wanted to tell them what had happened to him over the last month. The job offer. His new friend, Jack. The church he had been attending. He had so much to say, if only he could find Natalie and the girls to say it to.

"You look like a man in need of a friend." Jack Pace's warm voice pierced Mark's worried musings. Glancing at the envelope in Mark's hand, Jack shook his head. "Still no luck finding them? Maybe you should go up there and see what you can find out."

"I'm still a probationary employee at Whitneys. I've been looking for an engineering job for longer than I can tell you. How would it look if I took off after two weeks on the job? No." Mark vehemently shook his head. "I can't risk losing this opportunity. Besides, they've got me working around the clock."

"Son, you don't know they would fire you. Maybe if you explained your situation, they'd give you some time off."

Mark refused to even consider the notion. "No way. If you had been through what I have the last couple of years, you wouldn't risk losing your position, either. I am not going to make waves."

Jack shook his head, obviously concerned. "I know how important this job is to you, but what about your family?"

Mark looked him square in the eye, jaw set and voice raised. "This is about my family. Keeping this job is going to put food on their table and clothes on their backs. It is all about my family."

The silence that followed hung as dense as the fog that surrounded the two men. When Mark spoke again, his voice had lowered in volume and intensity. "Can you imagine if I did go? What would I tell Natalie? 'Yes, honey, I had a great job but lost it coming up to Seattle. In other words, we're right back where we started before I left.' No, thanks." The laugh that followed was forced and humorless.

Jack responded gently. "Mark, I don't have all the answers, but I know the Lord does. Maybe He can help you decide what to do." Jack glanced up at the ornate wooden church doors in front of them and then down at his watch. "In the meantime, if we don't get moving, we're going to miss out on serving dinner at the soup kitchen."

Despite his worries and frustrations about his own family, Mark had found that volunteering to serve meals to Eugene's homeless community brought him a peace that defied his circumstances. The church had started the program years before, and it had progressively grown from a few families fed in the church kitchen to more than one hundred people who filled a newly built cultural hall. Every evening, scores of volunteers amassed, cooking for and serving the ever-increasing number of hungry from the community. Recently, the halls had been filled with an inordinate number of elderly who had been forced to choose between much-needed medications and food. Even when the food bank couldn't keep up with the demand, the church always managed to.

"Soup kitchen" hardly described the spread that was furnished each evening. Jack's pet name for the feast, "the loaves and fishes dinner," had stuck, much to the congregation's delight. Even those in the community who had never cracked open a Bible knew that, often, the food at the Community Church's table had been stretched far beyond what could be explained in earthly terms.

Tonight, scanning the large crowd he was serving, Mark's gaze fell upon a young man holding a small baby. Two little girls clamored about his legs. Sudden longing pierced Mark's heart. What he would give for the embrace of his two sweet children.

After wrapping up his serving duties, Mark approached the man. Extending his hand, he warmly smiled. "Mark Thorsett."

The man gently returned the grin. "Evan Strong. I'd take your hand, but as you can see, mine are both in use."

Mark laughed aloud, looking down at the two girls hanging on the arm the baby was not in. "I've been there. I have two girls of my own."

The smallest child released her dad's arm and grabbed Mark's hand. Staring at him with bright blue eyes, she asked, "Are your girls here?"

"No. They aren't with me tonight." Mark shifted uncomfortably, not sure where the questions were headed.

"Are they at the shelter?" Innocence infused the question.

"No, honey. They are in Seattle."

If the child thought it strange that the children and dad were not together, she gave no indication. "We live at the shelter."

Mark managed to hide his shock. "You live at a shelter?"

"Yes. We used to have a house with just our family, but now we get to live with a lot of people. It's not too bad, except when they let the really noisy snorers in. They wake up the baby." The small girl rolled her eyes at Mark.

Mark caught Evan's gaze, who smiled back at him. "After my wife died a couple of months ago, I went into a deep depression. I missed a couple of shifts and lost my job. I suppose for most people that isn't a big deal, but when you're living paycheck to paycheck, one missed check can put you under."

Evan paused to muss his eldest girl's hair, who still silently clung to his leg. "The girls and I don't mind, though. Getting evicted gave me the wake-up call I needed. It kicked me out of the depression. I realized how much I still have to be grateful for." Evan's voice caught, emotions brimming. "These girls are the most incredible gifts from heaven, and I am the most blessed man on the earth."

Mark and Evan talked for another few minutes before the Strong girls hugged Mark and announced it was time to go. Watching the departing family, Mark was subdued. Even Jack's normal banter couldn't draw Mark out of his contemplative state. How could the homeless man be so upbeat? How could he be so peaceful? The man's words reverberated in Mark's head all night long. "I am the most blessed man on earth."

His brief spurts of slumber were restless at best. Self-posed questions reverberated in his head. No matter how many times they spun around, they remained unanswered. Had his wife grown so disgusted with his attitude and inability to provide that she'd deserted him? He wouldn't blame her. He had been a royal pill, but something deep inside told him that wasn't the case. Unfortunately, that same voice also told him things weren't well with his three Thorsett gals.

After hours of fighting a losing battle with the sandman, Mark rolled out of bed and knelt down. "Father, I know I've kind of fallen off the faith wagon, but I'm trying to get back on. I can't be home to watch over my family. I don't even know where they are. I know my kids desperately need a father. Right now I can't be there. Will you do double duty as their Father for me, until I can make it home? Please. And Father, could You maybe point me to the answers Evan Strong found? I think I could use them. In Jesus' name, amen."

Mark's prayer didn't bring closure to the reverberating questions, but peace, like a warm blanket, drew him into sleep.

CHAPTER 7

Natalie awakened early Saturday morning to the sounds of giggling children. Prying her eyes open, she spied pajama-clad Mollie and Amber laughing with two other children on the floor. As she sat up, she could see they were playing with handmade paper dolls. Some of the dolls were covered in colored advertising newsprint and junk-mail clothes, but the girls were obviously enjoying themselves. As Natalie observed the children, she realized they were as happy with the "fake" dolls as they had been with the plethora of store-bought dolls that had resided in the Thorsett home in the past.

"I wish we adults were as adaptable as those kids," Natalie muttered to herself.

"You got that right, sister."

Natalie turned abruptly, startled by the voice that came from her side. From the cot next to her, a six-foot-tall black woman unfolded herself from the makeshift covers.

Natalie smiled at her neighbor and then made a mental note. *Do not speak thoughts here that I intend to keep private.*

Her lesson learned was confirmed as the line of women emerging from cots and preparing for the day soon were engaged in animated conversation about the adaptability of children.

Her bunkmate laughed a deep belly laugh before verbally reiterating the lesson. "First thing you learn around here is that in close quarters, anything you say becomes fodder for conversation." She extended her hand. "Name's Sue. I'm on loan here from the domestic violence center down the road. They were full booked up last time Lloyd did a number on me. Dear El opened her doors and told me to stay until I could get my wounds healed and senses together." She looked at Natalie and then the girls. "What's your story?"

"Evicted." Natalie wasn't sure how open she wanted to be with the details of her life.

"Got a man?"

"Yes." Once again, Natalie provided only the most minimal response required.

"What's he like?"

Natalie turned and caught a glimpse of the wounded spirit in the eyes of the tough-looking woman next to her. She took a deep breath, then responded. "Mark's a good man. He's a great father. He's got the gentlest hands I've ever seen. I used to look at them and wonder if perhaps Jesus' hands were a little like his. Sometimes he's like a little boy — his excitement at Christmas. His play with the girls." Natalie had to stop as an incredible longing for her dear husband filled her and threatened to overflow.

Silence hung as Sue stared down at the cot. "I wish my man had gentle hands." The woman's body shook with the kind of grief that left no tear unshed.

Natalie searched for words but came up empty. Suddenly, she knew exactly what she should do. Taking the heirloom quilt off the bed, she took it over and wrapped it around the thin arms of the woman next to her. Before long, the shaking subsided.

Sue began to speak, blanket still held tightly around her shoulders. "El says I just need to use the courage and sense I have. Sometimes I don't feel like I have enough. Funny thing, though. Right now, I feel like maybe there's more down there than I know. Maybe there is some reserves in me."

Natalie uncharacteristically reached over and grabbed the woman's hand. "You know, if there is one thing I have learned lately, it's that when my strength falters, the Lord will fill in. 'I can do all things through Christ which strengtheneth me.' He's filled in for me, and I absolutely know He can strengthen you." Natalie was shocked by her own words. While she was definitely a believer in Christ, a Bible-quoting, testifying witness she was not. Had she gone over the line and offended this woman?

Sue lifted the blanket from around her and placed it gently back in Natalie's lap. She gazed at Natalie, tears brimming in eyes that bespoke years of pain. "I never been much of a church nut, but I think you are onto something. When you said those things, I knew you weren't just all talk." Pointing to her heart, Sue continued. "I felt something here."

"That's Him," Natalie whispered. "And He will never leave you or forsake you. I promise."

The women were interrupted by Amber's and Mollie's voices begging for breakfast.

Embracing both girls, Natalie kissed them and directed them to layer their clothes for the day. At El's directive, she loaded their belongings into the bag to haul along with her.

"Desperate times will drive even the purest heart to temptation, child," El had warned with a wink. "Hold on to what you have."

After Sue declined to join them, the three Thorsett girls headed for the dining area and the waiting oatmeal.

El approached Mollie and Amber, white teeth glowing. "Are you guys going to be my ladies-in-waiting today while your mama goes and tries to find herself a good job?"

Excited affirmations followed. As the girls finished their sugar-laden porridge, El took Natalie aside. Handing her a piece of paper, she cautioned, "Now when they ask you for an address on an application, you are going to have to put down something. Putting no address is an invitation for denial. I've given you my home address. You just put that down." Looking at the large sack of belongings on the floor, she winked and added, "And I'll keep those in my office. It wouldn't do you any good announcing to the world you are carrying your earthly wealth on your shoulders."

Natalie shook her head. "El, you've done so much for us already. You don't have to do this."

"Child, this is nothing. I just wish I could do more. Now, you take as long as you need. Little Miss Mollie and Miss Amber will be in good hands here." El's brows furrowed a bit when she added, "And Natalie, be careful. There are some awfully mean critters out there on the street. Watch your step."

Natalie hugged El and the girls, bundled into her coat, and set out for the central Pike Place Market area. The post-Christmas season was not the friendliest for any job seeker, especially a homeless woman with two children. Day care was out of the question — far too costly to support on close to minimum wage — so flexible hours were a must. By the end of her search, however, Natalie had ceased to mention anything about children, hours, or place of residence, hopeful for any employment. Discouragement nipped at her, as did the frosty late-afternoon air. *One day of this and I'm already feeling like a failure. No wonder Mark struggled after doing this for two years.* Understanding filled her, but the guilt that accompanied it only weighed more heavily on her burdened soul. *Why wasn't I more supportive? Why did I nag?*

Caught up in her own thoughts, Natalie failed to notice she had wandered past the street the shelter was on. Glancing around, she suddenly felt a sense of foreboding. The feeling turned to outright terror when a hand gripped her arm.

"Well, pretty lady, what a coincidence — and you thought we'd never meet again." The chillingly familiar voice gripped her intestines like a vise. "It must be destiny."

Natalie twisted around, desperately looking for an avenue of escape. Unfamiliar streets taunted her, and the industrial buildings about her seemed to have no entryways or people inside. She uttered an internal prayer for help and then faced Kinsey square on. "Kindly take your hand off me."

The expressionless face that stared back twisted into a sardonic grin. "Why, of course, my lady. Your wish is my command." His handgrip on her arm only tightened, however.

Once again, Natalie closed her eyes and prayed for help.

"Nobody's gonna hear those prayers down here, little lady. This ain't His territory." Kinsey laughed maniacally.

Suddenly, from around the corner, a yellow lab ran toward the two of them.

"Oh, look, a dog in shining armor," Kinsey joked, his eyes showing no humor.

Natalie watched in surprise as the seemingly tame, gentle creature, tongue lolling, approached them, then forcefully lunged at Kinsey. Grabbing the man's arm in his great jaws, the dog broke the connection between

Kinsey's hand and Natalie's arm. Freed, Natalie took off for the shelter as fast as her legs would carry her. Only after she was safely inside its doors did she pause to send a word of thanks upward.

Between labored breaths, she whispered, "Father, thank You. Thank You for all the things I took for granted and should have thanked You for long ago. A warm bed. A roof over our heads. Knowing You. My family. Safety. Mark. And thank You for all the recent times You've been there for me and with me. I love You, Lord. Oh, and I especially thank You for quilts and dogs."

Her prayer was interrupted when Amber and Mollie came around the corner and peppered her with questions. "How was your day?" "Did you get a job?" "Did you know we got to help stir the soup and press the biscuits for dinner?" Busy answering the girls, Natalie was left with little time to worry about the events of the day. If El felt something was out of the ordinary, she kept her mouth shut.

Before bed that night, Natalie cozied up under the covers with the girls. The bed Sue had occupied the night before was vacant. Natalie silently sent her off. *God bless you, Sue . . . and all the many others like you out there who have never known the warm, loving arms of a husband, or of a heavenly Father. May you find your way home soon.*

Late into the night the girls whispered stories of those they had met that day. A blind woman who played the accordion on the corner each day with her dog, hoping for enough money to pay for food and shelter. A family who had been burned out of their home and had not had adequate insurance. A mother and son who had been forced onto the streets after medical bills for a terminally ill child had mounted.

Amber reached over and gently stroked her mother's cheek. "You know, Mom, I never realized how lucky we are. I think we should have a family prayer to thank God."

Natalie nodded and softly whispered to her daughter to go ahead. The sweet words of the seven-year-old brought silent tears to her mom's eyes. She thanked the Lord for sight, for health, for their "new home" and Mama El, and for her family. She prayed for each person she had met that day and for those who weren't as lucky as Amber's family, having no nice, warm place to sleep that night. She concluded her prayer, "And Father, please bless my mom, that she might be safe and find a job. And bless my dad. Bring him home to be with us. We need him." Natalie and the girls fell asleep wrapped in the heirloom quilt that held their tattered lives and remnants of faith together.

CHAPTER 8

Mark Thorsett bolted out of bed, his heart pounding like a jackhammer. Sweat drenched his brow and trickled down his neck. He shook his head, trying to banish the visions that lingered from the all-too-real nightmare. Natalie was in danger. He rose and headed for the fridge, hoping a snack and glass of milk might counter the adrenaline coursing through his veins.

"Dreams are not reality," he said out loud, but the sound of the words failed to convince the rest of his body of the statement's truthfulness.

Shaking, he closed his eyes. Natalie was in a dark alley. She was looking around, terror etched on her face. Something was in the alley with her. Mark couldn't see what or who it was, but he could feel something. Whatever was on the brick-lined street with his sweet wife did not have good intentions. A sense of foreboding weighed on Mark like damp fog. Dream or not, he could tangibly feel the evil that had spurred him abruptly awake.

"What did I eat for dinner last night?" Mark shook his head, trying to figure out what gastronomic misstep had landed him in the world of indigestion that generated bad dreams.

One by one, he analyzed his food choices. "Ham sandwich, milk, bowl of tomato soup, salad, large piece of chocolate cake." At the cake, Mark paused. "That's it. It must have been the double-layer devil's food."

Swearing off pre-twilight sweets, Mark chalked up the unpleasant night as a lesson well learned and began his morning preparations for the day ahead.

Even with his concerns allayed, Mark still added a precautionary postscript to his early morning prayers. "Heavenly Father, be with Talie. I can't. She needs You. I know I certainly do. Keep her safe and protect her from evil. In Jesus' name, amen."

After finalizing his prework ritual, Mark sat down for a hurried breakfast. Despite finding the explanation for his early morning terror, he was having difficulty shaking the images and the uneasy feeling that lingered.

"Paranoia. That's what a large slice of

chocolate cake, coupled with a bit of worry about finding where Natalie and the girls have gone, will do to your imagination." He added, "Besides, now she is in our heavenly Father's hands — she's better off there than in mine." Even as Mark said the words, however, he was not entirely convinced.

Throughout the day, images from his predawn visions kept him unwelcome company. Pictures of Natalie's terror-stricken face danced across his computer whenever he had any downtime. Mark threw himself into his work, determined to drive out any space for unwanted images.

At the end of a long, exhausting day, Mark dragged himself down to Community's Soup Kitchen. Rushing to his serving place before the hungry hordes amassed for what would be the day's only meal for many of them, Mark only had time to quickly nod in Jack Pace's direction.

The line tonight seemed much longer than usual. As Mark dolled out large clumps of mashed potatoes, he was particularly drawn to the faces of the women and children. Had they always looked so gaunt? How had he missed the fear and concern etched in the mothers' countenances? Wherever his wife and children were, he was glad they had not fallen prey to the streets that aged these young souls far beyond their years.

One young woman approached him with two little boys. She appeared to have barely made it into adulthood. How old could she be? Nineteen? Twenty? And that was being generous. As he went to place the potatoes on her plate, his gaze met hers. The raw pain her emerald green eyes contained caught Mark's breath.

"Please, sir. Don't mind me. Could you give my portion to the boys?"

Her pleading tone and selfless gesture touched Mark's heart. "Ma'am, we have plenty here for everyone."

The woman shook her head. "But if I give my boys mine, they can have more, right?"

Mark gently placed his free arm on the woman's. The bone he felt seemed to be covered by little more than a layer of skin. "There is enough for all. You need your strength, too." Mark paused, then felt compelled to continue. Words flowed from a source seemingly outside of him. "It doesn't matter what has brought you here. It doesn't matter what you have done or how low you have sunk. You are loved. Your Father in heaven is intimately aware of you and Devon and Charlie. Katie, He loves you. He wants you to come home."

Tears flowed down the young woman's

cheeks like floodwaters. "How did you know our names?" she stammered through sobs.

Mark, for the first time, realized he had used their names. Not quite sure himself what had happened, he simply shook his head in wonder. "Our Father knows everything. Go home, Katie. Go home to your family. You will be welcome."

Reaching across the vat of potatoes, the teenager gave Mark a tearful, bony hug. "Thank you. You have no idea how hard it has been."

Mark nodded quietly, knowing she was right. Piling huge mounds of spuds on the plates of the small family, Mark heard his own words reverberating in his head. "Doesn't matter what you have done . . . how low you've sunk . . . He wants you to come home. . . . Go home to your family."

Were those words designed for someone besides Katie? Was God sending him a message, as well? Why else would He have chosen someone as imperfect and tainted as Mark to deliver His message to the young girl? Mark didn't know the answers, but he knew someone who would have them.

Long after every person in line had been fed and the last dishes were done, Mark and Jack Pace sat down to their own meals. Mark reviewed the evening's events with

Jack, then waited for his interpretation. To his disappointment, Jack declined.

"Mark, I've made my share of mistakes. I have learned over this long life, however, that when God communicates with someone, He is talking to that person alone. I can tell you what I think, but what good would that do? He didn't talk to me; He talked to you. If you have questions, ask Him." Jack's eyes twinkled as he winked at Mark. "Not that I don't love to put my two cents in every chance I get, but this is one I don't have the answers for."

Mark's frustration mounted. How could Jack not know? He was the most spiritually grounded person Mark knew. Having struck out in his attempt to get help with his experience earlier in the evening, Mark debated not bringing up his dreams at all. Curiosity won the debate, though, and Mark cleared his throat.

"Well, since you're not giving advice in the miraculous-communication-from-God department, how would you like to try the bad-food-induced-dream department?" Mark chuckled, hoping to lighten the memories of the morning's musings.

Jack raised an eyebrow. "Dreams and promptings from God. Wow, He must really be trying to tell you something." He smiled.

"Go ahead, son."

"Well, I had this large piece of chocolate cake a couple hours before I went to bed, and —"

Jack interrupted. "Get to the dream, boy. I don't need to hear how you blew your diet."

"It was Natalie. She was in trouble. Scared. Alone. Something really bad was after her. That's it. I don't know what it was or anything else. I don't even know where she was."

"What do you think it meant?" Jack said, flipping the question back to Mark as quickly as a short Ping-Pong rally.

"I've thought about it all day. I think my bad food choices and my inability to contact my family the last few weeks collided and produced a monstrosity of a dream." Mark looked at Jack, hoping for validation.

"You recall the story of Samuel?" Jack queried.

"Not sure. You want to give me the Cliffs-Notes version?"

"Samuel was a young man placed in Eli's charge at the tabernacle. One night he awakened, hearing a voice calling his name. He went to Eli to inquire what he desired, but Eli said it wasn't him calling. Twice more the voice came. Twice more he went to Eli. Eli finally perceived it might be the Lord and told Samuel that when the voice came again, to say, 'Speak, Lord; for thy servant heareth.' On the fourth occasion, Samuel did as he was told, and the Lord called him to be His servant and gave him a message."

Mark looked at Jack incredulously. "You can't be saying what I think you are. God spoke to Samuel. I didn't hear any voices."

"Son, God speaks in a multitude of ways. Some people see visions. Some dream dreams. Some hear voices. Some feel a warm feeling in their bosoms." Jack looked at Mark gently. "I'd say between what happened this morning and what happened this evening, you ought to ask Him what He would have you do."

"But if He wants me to go back up to Seattle, what will happen with my engineering job? I'm still on probation." Mark knew his face displayed intense fear. Letting go of the job he had searched years to find was unthinkable.

Jack placed his hand on Mark's shoulder. "If God asks you to go, He will provide a way."

Mark prayed long into the night. His evening pleadings began with the caveat, "I will go if You will find a way for me to keep my job." The peace that settled on Mark during his heavenly communications wrought a mighty change in his heart. By midnight, Mark had eliminated any conditions and changed his plea: "I will go if You want me to. Just keep my family safe. I can't bear the thought of something happening to them."

A repeat of the former night's performance left Mark with no doubt where he needed to be. Drenched in sweat once again, his beloved Natalie's terrified expression lingered in his mind.

He sat bolt upright, adrenaline pulsing. Clearly and decisively, Mark blurted, "I will go. Immediately. But where is she? And will I be there in time?"

CHAPTER 9

El shook her black curls and stared down at "her" sweet babies, Mollie and Amber, then back up at their mom. "Natalie, I am so sorry, child. I've tried everything I can to buck the red tape and get you an extension here. Nothing doing." Disgust emanated from her large body. "Those fancy-dancy office-bound decision-makers haven't had a night out in the cold their entire lives. What do they know about anything?"

Natalie sat silently as the words sank in. After three weeks, their time at the shelter was up. El had managed to buy them an extra week by burying their paperwork, but the powers that be had found it and were insisting the Thorsett family be tossed out. El's crescendoing voice caught Natalie's attention.

"Imagine a bunch of bureaucrats thinking they can tell me what I can do with my own home. They said taking you all into my place was some sort of conflict of interest. They don't know nothing about interest, except maybe a lack of it. And here you are not having no job yet, and these sweet babies need protection and warmth. It's criminal." El's stomped foot punctuated her feelings and reverberated across the wood floor.

"How long do we have?" Natalie's voice sounded thin and frail, even to her.

"Tomorrow, honey. Tonight will have to be your last night." El lowered her voice and looked around. "And you'll have to spend it in my office. They don't exactly know you're gonna be here. They are sending their inspector goons over first thing in the morning."

Even in the midst of her fear, Natalie felt gratitude for the woman whose heart matched her massive body in size. "Thank you so much for what you've done for us. I understand. There are a lot of homeless women and children needing the beds here. We've already had more time than we should have."

"Until they provide enough shelters to meet the demand, they ought not be coming in here and spouting off about building codes and capacities," El stormed. "Who cares about some building code when babies are dying on the streets from exposure?"

"Oh, Mama El, we'll be okay." Amber stretched her arms around part of El's middle. "Don't you worry. We won't be cold. We have each other and our special quilt. It will keep us warm and safe."

Amber's words triggered El's tear ducts. Large round drops coursed down her cheeks. Gathering the two girls in her arms, she gently rocked and nodded. "I reckon you're right, child. I reckon you're right."

Later, after the girls had been set to the task of preparing supper, Natalie had a chance to talk privately with El.

"So, what are our options?" Natalie queried.

"I checked with the local tent city. It's moved again, way up north. Too far for you to track down a job. All the other shelters are full. The domestic-violence homes are full up, too. I've got my feelers out, but nothing's coming back good." El placed her arm around Natalie's shoulders before heading to the kitchen to help the girls. "Something will work out. Don't you worry."

Natalie closed her eyes, hoping inspiration would hit her. The three weeks had flown by. Days of fruitless job searching followed by nights of restless sleep. The staff at the shelter had adopted Amber and Mollie.

Each morning one of them would faithfully take the girls to the bus stop, and each afternoon the girls would be picked up as Natalie tried to find employment. Despite the hardship and fear, the last three weeks had also opened Natalie's eyes to her many blessings. The revolving shelter door had brought her in contact with scores of women and children whose lives had been far more tumultuous and difficult than she could have imagined.

Some stories brought her to open tears as she tried to comfort wounded hearts and souls. The magnitude of sorrow and suffering in the world astonished her. She hadn't purposefully turned a blind eye to it. She had been involved with charities and had donated their family's used clothes. They had all volunteered for community work. And Natalie had been involved in her church. But she had no clue, not an inkling of understanding, how widespread and deep were the wounds that affected so many.

Despite having fewer temporal blessings than at any other time in her life, Natalie found herself more thankful for what she did have. Each night found the girls and Natalie on their knees in gratitude for all their blessings.

Natalie had been especially grateful for

her relationship with her heavenly Father over the last few weeks. She had come to rely heavily on His direction and still, small voice when looking for a job. Almost daily she had been directed down a certain street or away from a certain area. Such direction had saved her from any further encounters with Kinsey.

"Perhaps he's moved on," she hoped fervently.

The last couple of weeks had also provided key insight into her husband's world. Nothing in her life had prepared her for the feelings of inadequacy and dread that came from not being able to provide basic needs for her children. The fear hung over her head like a vulture and constantly threatened to send her into an emotional abyss of guilt and depression. She knew only too clearly how such feelings ate away at one's self-esteem.

I've only been at this a few weeks, she thought. *Mark's been dealing with it for years.* Gratitude for her husband's strength coursed through her. If only he were here.

Natalie went to join the girls in the kitchen, hoping the culinary work would take her mind off the looming deadline.

Entering the small space, Natalie saw her two girls, elbow deep in bread dough. "Hey,

Mom. We're kneading." Amber's smile spread dimple to dimple.

"I can see that. Any room for another set of hands?" The girls' positive response reflected how long it had been since their mom had been available to join them in activities. Her tireless dawn-to-dusk job search had taken her away from the girls, as well. Side by side with them at the kitchen counter, Natalie caught up with their lives. It almost felt like old times, when the three of them would bake fresh bread to welcome Mark home from a long day of work.

After the discussion had touched on a wide variety of subjects, Amber spoke. "Mom, we'll be okay, won't we?"

Natalie took Amber's face in her flour-dusted, dough-covered hands. "Sweetheart, we will be just fine."

Amber gazed thoughtfully back into her mother's eyes, while Mollie watched attentively. "Maybe Dad will come back and find a place for us."

The statement caught Natalie off guard. "We'll see, honey." Despite her ambiguous answer, Natalie knew the likelihood of that happening was close to none.

That evening as the girls prepared to sleep in El's office, Natalie thanked God they had been able to stay in the shelter for as long as they had, then said a silent prayer that they would have a place to stay the next night. Despite being pitched to and fro in a sea of unknowns, the heirloom quilt guided the three Thorsetts safely into the dream world.

The next morning dawned bright, cold, and far too early for Natalie's liking. A small group of staff gathered to bid the Thorsett family a tearful good-bye. Offers to stop by for lunch and dinner were extended by El out of earshot of the arriving officials. She pressed an address into Natalie's hand. "I've got a friend who owns a restaurant downtown. He's got a large storage area in the alley off the back of the shop. It's not heated, but it's covered and has four walls. He said you guys can camp there for a couple of days." She wiped a tear away. "I wish I could do more. I'll keep my ear to the ground."

She grabbed the girls in a tearful embrace as they were drawn into the soft folds of her body. "You take care of your mommy, Miss Amber and Miss Mollie, you hear me? Or Mama El will come and give you what-for."

She handed each girl a package loaded with food and treats before she turned to Natalie. "Let me help you get this." El lugged Natalie's belongings up and onto her back. Poking out the top were bags of food and items El had clumsily shoved in.

"Thanks, El. For everything." Natalie gave the large woman a hug, and the three Thorsett girls walked out onto the chilly street.

The day was spent hanging around shops in the downtown corridor. Pike Place offered some indoor areas where the family walked as unobtrusively as possible, trying to stay warm. Natalie was amazed at how many other people she recognized from the shelter. *I've been to Pike Place dozens of times before. Why didn't I see all of these homeless people?*

Occasionally a shopkeeper would ask them to leave, but by and large they welcomed the little girls and their mother. Aromas assaulted them almost cruelly, tempting of goodies and treats out of reach. French baked goods. Russian filled pastries. Stuffed pork humbow. Natalie tried to steer the girls away from the vendors, but both Amber and Mollie begged. "Oh, Mom — even if we can't eat them, we can smell them and dream."

As evening approached, Natalie was reluctant to leave the crowded but safe market for the address that lay buried in her pocket. She bundled the girls around her and headed in the direction El had indicated. After blocks of walking, they approached the marked alleyway. Darkness cast shadows across the bricks. Even the usually cheerful girls looked at the black corridor with concern.

"Are you sure we have the right place?" Mollie asked timidly.

Natalie attempted to put on a happy face, hesitant to step from the relative protection of the streetlights into the unknown. "Remember, girls, as soon as we get safely inside, we have the flashlight El gave us and the book she sent along. We also have Daddy's Bible. We'll read together. I think she may even have thrown in some cookies."

With the promise of cookies, the girls tentatively followed Natalie into the alleyway. Passing three closed metal doorways and a Dumpster, Natalie came to a large metal door with the numbers 6064 scrawled in black paint. Graffiti lined the walls with symbols and letters unfamiliar to her. She reached the door and turned the knob; the door opened into a pitch-black room. Grabbing the flashlight from her bag, she shone it around the small space. The concrete floor had not been cleaned in some time, and the plywood walls were lined with cardboard boxes. It was not pretty, but it was better than the street. Natalie herded the girls in, then quickly shut the door behind them.

She reached to lock the door but fumbled trying to find it. Shining the light on the door, she came to an extremely unpleasant realization; it had no lock. She struggled to put on a brave face for the girls, hoping they weren't aware of what she'd learned. "So, who's up for some story time and cookies?" She layered the girls in all their clothes and then wrapped the quilt around all three sets of shoulders. In the darkness, illuminated only by the small flashlight, the quilt brought a measure of peace as they read from the picture book and Bible.

Tired from their long day at the market and exposure to the elements, the girls fell asleep immediately. Natalie was glad. Seattle was not a calm place at night. Loud voices and laughter filled the small room as people cut through the alley. Some seemed to be coming home from dinner or parties. Others sounded more ominous. The threats and obscene language of gangs. The clatter of other homeless people, searching through the Dumpster for food. Even within the folds of the quilt, Natalie couldn't sleep; she was only too aware of the girls by her side.

Finally she drifted into a fitful rest, giving in to the effects of the physically and emotionally exhausting day. In the early morning hours Natalie was awakened by a sound she hadn't heard before — a slow shuffling. Someone was searching the alley. *But what could they be looking for?* Terror gripped Natalie as the footsteps stopped outside the door. Despite the thin metal barrier separating her from the alleyway, Natalie could feel a presence on the other side. She didn't need to see what was out there to know its intentions. The evil that permeated the small room where she and the girls lay was palpable. She silently reached out and placed a hand on the Bible. Her other hand stroked the quilt. After what seemed like hours, the steps moved on down the alley.

Natalie breathed a sigh of relief. She and the girls had dodged a bullet tonight, but how many more nights would they have? "Oh, Father, send help," she whispered. "And please send it soon."

CHAPTER 10

Light stretched slender fingers under the door and gently awakened the Thorsett girls. Amber yawned and sat up. "Boy, Mom. I thought the bed at the old apartment was hard. This floor is hard as concrete!"

Natalie smiled. "That's because it is concrete." Both girls laughed. In the daylight their surroundings didn't seem nearly as ominous as they had the night before.

Still, Natalie quickly set about gathering their possessions and loading them into her bag. They would sleep here out of necessity, but she wasn't going to stick around during the day. Home sweet home this was not. She scouted the alley before leaving the room. Lessons from last night lingered. She would make every effort to enter and exit their sleeping quarters in as inconspicuous a manner as possible. No need to call unwanted attention to themselves. It seemed unnatural to have the weight of her children's safety resting solely on her shoulders. How she longed for her husband's much broader shoulders to help carry the load. In fact, right now there was no place she would rather be than in the safe and loving embrace of his arms. "Regrets won't get me anywhere this morning," she muttered before heading down the corridor back to the main street.

While normally not a supporter of Sunday shopping, Natalie was glad the stores were open this day. They offered needed warmth from the chilly winds. Ducking in and out with the girls, she managed to keep them semiwarm until they reached the shelter.

El had directed them to use the back door, in case any "official mucky mucks," as she termed them, were hanging around.

Natalie knocked three times and waited for an answer. El's curly mop poked out of the door. Eyes opened wide with pleasure and surprise, she corralled the clan into the small kitchen. "Land sakes, let's get you all out of that freezing cold." She met Natalie's gaze above the girls' heads.

"How was your night?"

"Okay." Natalie shook her head silently, conveying that the rest of the story would have to be out of earshot of the girls.

97

El obviously understood, as she put the girls to work making the bread for lunch. The promise of a warm afternoon spent in the shelter's kitchen, coupled with seeing El, made the girls almost giddy. Their laughter followed El and Natalie when they left the children under the watchful supervision of the shelter's cook.

Safe and alone in El's tiny office, she turned her piercing brown gaze on Natalie. "How was it?"

Natalie set forth the night's events, only this time she left nothing out.

El shook her head, worry clearly etched upon her face. "Most of this I've heard before. Gangs, transients looking for food. I knew you might see those things. But the person hanging around looking — that worries me. Did anyone see you go down the alley?"

Natalie shook her head, trying to remember. "I don't think so. I tried to be careful."

"I don't get it. What would somebody want in that alley? You had any problems like this before?"

Natalie dropped her gaze. "Well, I did have this one guy following me."

El's eyebrows shot up. "And who might that be?"

"Some guy named Kinsey." Natalie's

tongue almost spit the name out.

El's face bore an expression Natalie had never seen. "Oh, no, child. He's the worst of the worst. Bottom of the pile. Even the baddest down here stay clear away from him. How on earth did you get hooked up with him?"

Natalie relayed the story.

El pursed her lips. "I am coming down and staying with you-all tonight." Her tone offered no opportunity for argument.

The Thorsetts stayed as late into the evening as safety would allow, and then El, Natalie, and the children set out. El kept a careful eye peeled for those who might be following. Finally satisfied they had made the trip alone and unobserved, they opened the metal door and entered. The night was uneventful as they went through their story-and-cookie ritual and then wrapped up in the quilt. It managed to stretch to cover even El's oversized body. Kneeling, they each prayed. Mollie went last.

"And Lord, please keep us safe. And help Daddy find us. We need him." The chorus of amens was heartfelt and loud. Long after the girls and El had been overtaken by sleep, Natalie was repeating the words of her youngest daughter's prayers.

Natalie couldn't be sure what time it was

when something outside disturbed her sleep. The hair on her neck rose as if sleep-walking. Someone was in the alley. She didn't need anyone to tell her that this was a repeat performance of the night before. She gazed down at the sleeping trio on the floor, thankful that none of them were snorers.

As the steps moved down the alley away from her, Natalie braved a peek out the door. A tall, lean figure clad in black, its back to Natalie, made its way down the alley toward the Dumpster. It bent and stooped, searching every square inch. Then, turning his attention away from the Dumpster to the building behind it, the creature rattled each door and began working his way back down the alley. Doors with no locks were opened. Realization hit Natalie like a freight train. The person was determined to find what he was unable to learn last night and was methodically going through the alley to do it. It wouldn't be long until he reached the door that hid the Thorsett family and El.

Natalie glanced down at her small children wrapped safely in the patchwork quilt and knew what she had to do. If the figure continued, he would find them all. Natalie had to distract him. Quietly, she kissed each girl on the cheek and wrapped the quilt more tightly around them. She silently slid out the door and clicked it behind her. Praying for her safety and theirs, she took off running in the opposite direction, knowing full well her footsteps would notify the evil searcher of her presence.

She was right. She hadn't taken but a few strides when she heard the footsteps behind her give chase. Running for her life, she balanced her terror with the knowledge that the farther she could get away from door 6064, the farther this evil was from her sweet daughters. Twenty yards. Fifty yards. Then the street.

Terror pierced Natalie's soul when she found the street empty. What had she expected? It was the middle of the night. She knew she didn't have much longer before the odious footsteps caught up with her. She headed for the streetlight; if she were going to die, perhaps someone would see it happen.

Knowing he was close behind her did not prepare Natalie for the terror she experienced at the brutal grasp of the man's hand on her shoulder. Natalie knew the grip. She had felt it before.

Kinsey's panting voice rang with victory. "Don't suppose you have a dog handy tonight, do you?"

Without turning around, Natalie glanced at the hand gripping her shoulder. The dog had left deep marks in his hand, not yet fully healed. Natalie silently cheered.

With strength she didn't know she possessed, she turned and faced the gloating villain. "Who knows what my God has in store for you? Could be a dog. Could be an alligator. But rest assured, it will be something."

Kinsey's laugh reverberated down the empty street. "Oh yes. I can see, my beauty. He has a whole army here tonight to protect you." Grabbing her roughly, he pressed his lips to her ear and hissed, "It's just a shame He is going to be a little too late tonight." He underscored his statement by eerily whistling the familiar refrain from "Some Enchanted Evening."

Natalie struggled to break his grasp but couldn't. In a last-ditch effort, she looked up the sloping street and boldly announced, " 'I will lift up mine eyes unto the hills, from whence cometh my help. My help cometh from the Lord.' "

As if on cue, she saw a vision more beautiful than any dog she had ever seen. Cresting the hill and running at an all-out sprint was her husband, Mark Thorsett. Seeing the love of her life gave her power she didn't know she possessed. She sharply elbowed Kinsey in the solar plexus. The man's explosive exhale of air told her she had found her mark. As his grip relaxed, she jerked away and ran up the hill toward her husband.

"How did you find us?" she gasped.

"Later, Talie." The smile he gave her spoke more than any words as he hurled past her toward the waiting man. When he was finished with the man, Kinsey's face was expressionless no longer. Pain had replaced the evil intent that had filled Kinsey's eyes just moments earlier. The welcome wail of police sirens, followed by the arrival of the patrol unit, strobe lights flashing, allowed Mark to get off the man he had been sitting on. As they carted Kinsey off to jail, Mark looked down at his wife. Taking her in his arms, he lifted her chin to allow him to gaze fully into her eyes. "Fancy meeting you here, Mrs. Thorsett."

Natalie threw her arms around his neck and kissed him. Tears flowed down their cheeks as the two found themselves, by God's gentle grace, where they belonged — together.

"I have so much to tell you," Natalie blubbered.

Mark placed his finger gently on her lips, then said, "The same here. But later. Right now I just want to look at you. If you only knew how I've longed to see you. I am so sorry for not appreciating you when I had you, and for so many of the things I said and did."

It was Natalie's turn to quiet Mark. "It doesn't matter. None of it does. I realized it didn't matter where we were or what we had. As long as we were together as a family, it was enough. Job or no job, Mark Thorsett, we are going to follow you wherever you go."

The joyful reunion was interrupted by the sounds of young children. Propelling themselves down the alley under El's watchful eye were Amber and Mollie. "Daddy! Daddy!"

Mark lifted the girls in one motion. Holding them for what seemed an eternity, he reluctantly bent to put them back on the ground. Eyes full of merriment, he queried, "Isn't it past your bedtime?" The girls responded with giggles, obviously as much amused by the fact that their dad hadn't said anything about them being in the middle of the street in the wee dawn hours as they were by his comment.

"Oh, Daddy." Mollie wrapped herself

around his leg semipermanently. "Don't ever leave us again."

Mark tenderly knelt by both girls, under the tearful scrutiny of both Natalie and a blubbering El. "I won't. I promise." He took the girls' smallest fingers and wrapped them around his own. "Pinkie swear."

Mollie looked deep into her daddy's eyes, then asked, "How did you find us?"

Amber answered quietly. "Our heavenly Father told him where we were. I know He did. We prayed and He led Daddy to us."

Mark took Amber in his arms, noticing for the first time that his Bible was clutched firmly in her hands. "Amen to that, little girl. Amen to that."

Mollie added, "And we had faith you'd come back." She looked to her mom for reassurance that she had used the words correctly.

Natalie nodded, glancing at the quilt that El had wrapped around her shoulders. "We did have faith. Remnants of faith."

CHAPTER 11

Natalie Thorsett leaned her head against the window and let the sweet, warm rays of the morning sun stretch across her face. She kept her eyes shut, basking in the gentle snoring sounds that serenaded her from the adjacent hotel bed. The peaceful scene was a marked contrast to the tumultuous events of the preceding night. Natalie gazed at Mark, willing him to awaken so that she could obtain answers to her many questions. Last night she had been too caught up in the emotion of the events to question him, but today all the unasked questions begged a response.

Mark stirred, as if feeling her gaze upon him. His eyes opened. Catching sight of Natalie, a grin spread across his face. He leaped from the bed and vigorously embraced her. His joy was contagious.

Natalie waited for him to sit in the chair she had pulled to the window, then leaned back into his lap. Safe in his embrace, the questions came faster than the answers.

"How on earth did you find us? How did you manage to show up right when I needed you? Where have you been? Why didn't you respond to my letters?"

Mark interrupted Natalie's series of questions with a heartfelt laugh. Hands raised in defeat, he joked, "One at a time, one at a time. The way I see it, we have a whole lifetime ahead of us for me to answer all the questions you want to ask, so go easy on me.

"I guess I should start with the question about the letters," he continued. "I'm not sure what letters you are talking about, but my guess is I missed them. I moved so quickly from city to city in the beginning, I left no forwarding address. I wasn't sure where the letters needed to wind up. I'm sorry. I thought that even if you didn't know where I was, I knew where you would be when I sorted things out." He shook his head. "Boy, was I wrong.

"When I finally ended up in Eugene, Oregon, I wore out my phone lines and the lock on my post office box trying to find you." Taking her hands in his, Mark turned her around to face him and gazed deep into her eyes. "I am so sorry. I had no idea what you and the girls were going through. I was terribly wrong to leave. Can you ever forgive me?"

Natalie felt her eyes fill. "It's all right. I've learned to let it go. Now you need to." Gaining her composure, she squeezed his hand. "Eugene? What's in Eugene?"

"An engineering job . . . I think. At least there was a job until I came to Seattle to look for you guys." Mark smiled wryly.

Natalie couldn't believe her ears. "A job? You found a job?" She wrapped her arms around Mark's waist. "We're going to Eugene!"

"Yes, we are. But first you need to hear the rest of the story. I left Eugene a week ago. I went first to our old apartment. The new tenants knew nothing about you, and, as I'm sure you can guess, our dear old landlord wouldn't give me the time of day." Mark's face twisted in anger at mention of the man. "Finally, I camped out on his front porch for an entire day and threatened to stay there indefinitely if he didn't tell me everything he knew about where you were."

Mark smiled. "Let's just say he found me very persuasive. He told me about your three-day notice and how, as a Christmas present, he hadn't evicted you on the holiday. Other than that, he knew nothing."

Mark looked at his attentive listener. "If you had any idea what it did to me to think of you girls out there with no place to go . . ." Mark's voice choked with emotion as he continued. "I didn't know what to do. I just knew I needed to find you. After exhausting every other avenue I could think of — shelters, low-income housing, food banks, hospitals, even police stations, I finally went to the girls' school. After getting past all the red tape, I was able to talk to the principal, to their teachers, and finally to the bus driver who picked up the girls. She's the one who directed me to the stop last night. She told me which direction she normally saw the girls head and described the woman who sometimes would meet them."

He paused and grinned at Natalie. "I knew it had been awhile since I saw you, but it didn't take a rocket scientist to figure out the two-hundred-plus-pound African American woman who was picking them up was not you."

Natalie laughed at the loose description of El, then waited for Mark to continue. "Armed with her description, I spent last evening canvassing the streets trying to figure out who she might be. I felt a sense of urgency, an inner voice spurring me forward. I knew I couldn't wait until morning."

Natalie nodded. "I've become acquainted with that voice myself recently."

Mark and Natalie shared a moment of silent understanding; then Mark went on. "Close to midnight, I ran into a woman who thought she knew who I was talking about. She led me to the shelter. I must have awakened all the residents pounding on the door, but they didn't seem to care. They told me El had taken off with you guys for the night but would be back in the morning. I just knew I couldn't wait until then."

Natalie shivered. "Thank goodness you listened to the voice."

"You don't even know the half of it. I took off in the direction the lady indicated you had headed but didn't have a clue where you might be. Every intersection, every corner, I felt a hand propelling me forward and the voice in my head telling me which direction to go. Street after street. Each time I had to make a decision, I knew where to turn. At the end I was running as fast as my legs could carry me." Mark's eyes flowed freely at the memory. "It was the most miraculous experience I have ever had. It's funny, but when I crested the hill and headed down the street toward you, I felt no surprise you were there. I wasn't sure which street you would be on, but I knew the owner of the voice that was leading me did know."

Natalie opened her mouth but couldn't speak. She knew exactly who had led Mark to her. It was the One whose arms had encircled and protected her little family out on the cold streets and whose voice had whispered words of forgiveness and encouragement to her heart. And the One who had divinely directed a loving teacher to make a gift of a warm, protective quilt. Natalie buried her head in Mark's shoulder, thankful most of all that He had also healed her family's brokenness.

The rest of the year flew quickly by as the Thorsett family started anew. The move to Eugene was filled with great joy and anticipation. The happiness was magnified when they learned that Mark's job was securely his. Jack Pace became an adopted member of the family. Activities soon filled their lives. None, however, could compete with their once-a-week journey downtown to help feed Eugene's homeless population. Through the spring, summer, and fall, the Thorsetts became a symbol of hope to the people who came to receive physical nourishment, but often left spiritually and emotionally nourished, as well.

On Thanksgiving Day the Thorsett family once again headed for Community Church's familiar building. Amber had insisted on taking with them something she had secretly secured in a large plastic bag. Despite repeated questions from her parents, she refused to tell what was hidden inside. She and Mollie shared furtive glances and giggles over the obviously jointly hatched plan. Finally, after the meal had been served and grown-ups and children broke off into little conversational groups, the secret was revealed. Natalie watched as her daughters gathered the other children around them and pulled the heirloom quilt out of the bag. As each child touched the quilt, Natalie moved closer to hear what Amber was saying.

"Last year we were just like you. We didn't have our house or bed or anything. But when we were the saddest and most scared, that's when God sent us this quilt. Every time we felt bad or cold or afraid, we'd just put this around us and we could feel His arms holding us tight. He loves little children. I know He loves me, and I know He loves you guys, too. Even if you don't have anything else, you do have something to be thankful for — God. And His Son, Jesus. And maybe if you ask Him, He'll put His arms around you, too."

"Can we put the quilt around us?" The frail girl who spoke looked as if her own voice frightened her.

Amber and Mollie both gave her big smiles. "Yes," they responded in unison. Then Amber continued, "It won't be long until we have to give this quilt to someone else who needs it. The lady who sent it to us wanted us to give it to someone else, a man. Next week we're flying to Alaska to give it to him. But tonight, we wanted you guys to feel God's arms around you."

One by one, the motley group of children wrapped the folds of the quilt securely around their shoulders. Some closed their eyes when they pulled it around themselves. Others covered their heads in the warm cover. As the quilt passed by and everyone had a turn with it, each small child's face wore a peaceful smile. Though no longer in the quilt's embrace, its message clearly remained in the young hearts: You are loved.

ABOUT THE AUTHOR

Renee DeMarco is an award-winning, multi-published author and a practicing attorney. She has authored many beloved titles. Renee resides in Washington State with her husband and three daughters.

■ ■ ■ ■

SILVER LINING

BY COLLEEN L. REECE

■ ■ ■ ■

DEDICATION

To Eric, Kelly, and all those who
serve at home and overseas,
with special thanks to Ron Wanttaja
for additional resource material.

When I consider thy heavens,
the work of thy fingers,
the moon and the stars,
which thou hast ordained;
What is man, that thou art
mindful of him? . . .
[Thou] hast crowned him with
glory and honour.
PSALM 8:3–5

CHAPTER 1

Middle Eastern skies

"That's it for this time, Burgess Benjamin." Major Gavin Scott, U.S. Air Force Raven reconnaissance pilot, grinned broadly, anticipating his wiry, red-haired RSO's usual explosive response.

It wasn't long in coming. Captain Sharp bristled like a porcupine. "Once more with the Burgess and you'll be minus one RSO," he threatened. "I can claim mental anguish as grounds for a transfer." He grimaced. "Why anyone would hang a name like Burgess on an unsuspecting kid is beyond me. It took a dozen black eyes given and received before people got the message that I'm Ben."

Gavin wasn't through heckling his reconnaissance systems operator. Ignoring the oft-heard account of his best friend's woes, he shifted in his seat and accused, "Transfer? You? Fat chance. According to your bragging, I couldn't fly my way out of a paper bag without you." Laughter blossomed like a fully opened parachute.

"You couldn't," Ben retorted, but a grin spoiled his mock indignation.

Gavin felt his lips twitch. "Yeah, right. I do have to admit, though, you're as faithful as Patsy Ann."

"Patsy Ann?" Ben looked suspicious. "Who's she? An old girlfriend?" He brightened. "Hey, now that you're engaged to the foxy Christa Jensen Bishop, how about introducing me to your Patsy Ann? I don't like to talk about myself, but . . ." He threw out his chest and grinned again.

It was all Gavin could do to control his mirth. "No introductions. First, she's too old for you. Second, she's not your type. Third, the city of Juneau would declare war if you tried to take Patsy Ann away from them."

"Is this another one of your Alaskan tall tales? Like the one about the midair collision between a B-727 and a salmon?"

Temporarily distracted from his Patsy Ann story, Gavin shook his dark head. "According to the tour guides in Juneau, that really happened. I wasn't there, but they swear it's a matter of historical record. An eagle swooped down and caught a huge salmon.

Frightened by the noise, the eagle dropped it. Result: wing damage from the salmon — to the plane, not the eagle."

Ben smirked. "Sounds fishy to me."

Gavin groaned. "Do you want to hear about Patsy Ann or not?"

"Sure."

"Patsy Ann lived in Juneau in the 1930s."

Ben snorted. "A 70-something-year-old woman? Just my luck."

Gavin ignored him. "She died in 1942. She was so respected, a huge crowd came to say their farewells when her coffin was lowered into the Gastineau Channel." He paused. "I was really impressed the first time I saw Patsy Ann and heard her story."

"What do you mean, saw her? You weren't born until the mid-70s."

"A bronze statue was erected in Marine Park. Patsy Ann greets guests arriving in Juneau by sea, just as she did for so many years."

Ben shrugged. "What was she? The town hostess? Why did you say I was as faithful as she was?"

"You are. I'll tell you what I'm talking about." Gavin cleared his throat. "Dad was career military but retired after twenty years. We came back to Alaska after I finished second grade in Boise, Idaho. Dad didn't want me yanked in and out of differ-ent schools every time he got transferred." He fell silent. Homesickness for Alaska and the MacJean Flight Service owned and operated by his parents, Mackenzie and Jean Scott, assailed him. Anger followed. If it weren't for those driven by hatred and lust for power, he'd be home now. Yet fanat-ics must be stopped, even when it meant tearing men and women from their homes to defend their countries against terrorism.

"What does your dad's career have to do with Patsy Ann?" Ben asked.

"Everything. When Dad wasn't busy with charter flights, he took Mom and me all over Alaska. The first trip was to Juneau. I remember how beautiful it was, built against green mountains, with the Gastineau Channel between it and Douglas Island with its snowcapped mountains. The statue of Patsy Ann sat on the dock, looking out at the harbor. A plaque told her story, but Dad had already filled me in." He paused, feeling the same awe he had experi-enced as a child clinging to his father's strong hand.

Ben sighed. "It would be nice if you'd tell me, preferably sometime before I have a long white beard."

Gavin pulled out of his reverie. "Okay,

Burgess Benjamin. Patsy Ann was a bull terrier —"

"And I remind you of her? Thanks a lot." Ben's voice dripped with sarcasm.

Gavin grinned. "She was actually deaf and mute, unlike some people I know."

"So?" Ben bristled. "Is that supposed to make me feel better?"

"Wait till you hear the rest of the story, okay?" Gavin didn't wait for a reply. "No one knew how, but Patsy Ann could sense when a steamship was coming into the harbor. She always raced to meet it. Perhaps because return visitors brought her scraps from the ships' dining rooms — unlike today, when you can't take food off the ships. Whatever the reason, Patsy Ann never missed meeting a steamship."

"That's incredible." Ben sounded properly impressed.

A familiar tingling went through Gavin. He felt the same small-boy wonder that always accompanied the telling of the story. "It was incredible, but not so much as what happened later. A steamship was unable to dock at the usual place and time. It's not clear whether the reason was a storm or trouble aboard. Anyway, when the ship docked at a different place, long after expected, Patsy Ann was there to meet it."

"How do you explain that?"

Gavin shook his head. "No one can. It just happened. There are lots of things we can't explain. Only God understands the workings of His creation, including the intuition He placed in a deaf and mute dog's mind and heart."

"Not many people are as faithful as Patsy Ann." Ben sounded sad.

Gavin shot a quick look at his RSO, but Ben was staring straight ahead. No wonder. He had been a wishbone child, pulled between two sets of parents after a messy divorce. Sympathy softened Gavin's voice. "We can be glad God is faithful."

"Yeah." Ben hunched his shoulders. "Wonder what the flight schedules during the holidays will be? I'd sure like to be in the good old U.S. of A. for Christmas this year. Or at least for Thanksgiving." His voice turned somber. "I never knew how much I had to be thankful for until I came over here."

"You've got that right," Gavin agreed. Another wave of rage rose within him. Yet as long as wicked men chose evil over good and attempted to annihilate all those who disagreed with them, there would be conflict.

Gavin forced himself to quell his anger

and concentrate on his flying. A combat aircraft was no place for negative emotions. They could lessen a pilot's vigilance and lead to disaster.

Flying. How he loved it! His mind ran double track, split between the job at hand and his earliest memories. . . .

"Daddy, why can't I fly like the birds?" he asked one afternoon when they stood watching a pair of hawks lazily circling in the blue, blue sky. He flapped his arms, ran across the grassy yard of their home on a hillside just outside of Anchorage, and leaped in the air, only to come down in a hurry.

Strong arms caught him up and perched him on a muscular shoulder. Gray eyes like his own twinkled when Mackenzie Scott replied, "We have to be content to fly in airplanes, son. Someday, when you're old enough, I'll teach you. Your mother and I chose the Welsh name Gavin because it means 'white hawk.' "

Gavin squinted. "But, Daddy, our hawks aren't white."

His father laughed. "No, they aren't. White hawks live far, far away in places like southern Mexico and Central and South America. I'll show you those countries on the world map when we go inside."

"Do our hawks ever go visit the white ones?" Gavin inquired.

Mackenzie Scott shook his head. "It is much too far for them to fly."

"Someday I'll go where the white hawks are," the boy vowed. "I'll tell them our hawks are sorry they can't come see them."

"I won't be surprised." His father set him down. "Run and wash your hands. It's almost time for supper."

Late that night, father, mother, and son took a walk under the northern stars. On the way home, Gavin stood on tiptoe and stretched his arms into the air. "Mommy, if my arms were longer, I could pick a star for you," he announced.

Jean Scott's laughter rippled like a happy brook tumbling over stones on its way to the sea. "Which one would you pick?"

"Polaris. The North Star." A chubby finger unerringly pointed to the star located almost directly over the North Pole. "Daddy says it's 'portant to know how to find it, in case we get lost. First we find the Big Dipper." He moved his hand. "Then we draw a straight line from the 'pointer stars' to the end of the Little Dipper's handle."

"What if clouds cover the sky and you can't see the North Star?" Jean teased.

Gavin looked at her with wide eyes, thinking with all his might. A confident smile broke across his face. "Then you ask God to tell you which way to go." With a whoop of pure joy, he raced ahead of them toward the lighted windows that meant home and security. But he never forgot that night.

Shortly after Gavin and Ben completed their run and headed toward home base, disaster struck. One moment, the Raven steadily pursued its course. The next, the two men were surrounded with flashing lights and blaring warning horns. Gavin's lightning-quick glance at Ben's pale face and his fervent "God help us!" confirmed the problem — a major fire in the left engine compartment. A pilot's worst nightmare, especially when flying Middle Eastern skies.

Please God, not here, not now, Gavin silently pleaded. Summoning all his self-control, he turned off the fuel to the left engine and activated the fire-suppression system. No effect. The horns and lights doubled as fire spread to the right engine compartment. The metallic taste of fear filled his mouth. While Ben prayed and smoke started filling the cockpit, Gavin tried to stop the second fire. Yet despite prayer and Gavin's efforts, nothing worked.

The plane started to gyrate as hydraulic lines to the control surfaces burned away. He felt the thud of a small explosion just behind the cockpit.

A taunting voice hammered a message into Gavin's brain: *You are going to die. You'll never see Christa, your parents, or Alaska again.* A heartbeat later, a sharp blow to his head brought darkness, as complete and total as if every trace of light had been snatched from the earth by a giant, malevolent hand. The last thing he heard before sinking into its smothering depths was Ben's loud cry, "God, have mercy! Eject, eject, eject!"

Hours or centuries later, Gavin awoke to a world blacker than a starless, moonless night at sea. Dazed and disoriented, he felt a steady pressure on his head and something wet running down his face. He called out, "Dad? Did we have to ditch?" but no answer came.

"Gavin."

He struggled against the dizziness that held him against his will and finally managed to whisper, "Dad?"

"No, not your dad, Gavin. It's Ben. Wake up, Sleeping Beauty." The lightly chosen words didn't hide the gravity of his RSO's voice. "I did something to my ankle when we crashed. It isn't broken — torn ligaments, maybe. I can hobble, but I need your help. Do you hear me, Gavin? I need you. Now. We have to get out of here and find cover before unwelcome visitors come sniffing around the ejection capsule."

The urgency in Ben's voice, more than his words, brought Gavin fully alert. He reached up to his aching head but contacted Ben's hand.

"Don't touch your head — something struck you. Hard. I put a compress on the wound. Thank God it has stopped bleeding. We need to get going."

Gavin's tongue felt thick. "How can we find cover in this pitch-black darkness?" he snapped. A moment later, suspicion mingled with a stream of cold fear and raced up his spine.

"What do you mean, darkness?" Ben demanded.

The shock in his friend's voice turned suspicion to certainty. Gavin fought nausea, gritted his teeth, and ground out, "You're going to have to pilot this expedition, Ben." He hesitated, then hoarsely added, "I can't see."

CHAPTER 2

Anchorage, Alaska

Halfway around the world, twenty-six-year-old nurse-practitioner Christa Jensen Bishop finished the last-minute check of her well-stocked Ford Explorer, in preparation for another day's work. She paused to sniff the breeze ruffling the soft brown hair that had escaped from the hood of her scarlet parka. It was her favorite time of year — crisp, cold October. Brilliant sunlight. How she loved the snowcapped mountains. Their lofty, magnificent heads jutted thousands of feet into the cloudless sky behind Anchorage, and the sun-kissed water of Cook Inlet shimmered with a million golden motes.

Christa saluted the life-sized statue of British Captain James Cook nearby, where he had first anchored in 1778. What had he thought when he saw the site of what became a proud city? The municipality of Anchorage was one of only seven cities nationwide to have won the prestigious All-American City Award four or more times.

Christa's heart filled with gratitude. *Thank You, God. If it weren't for Susan . . .* She expertly switched her train of thought to the day ahead. The 150 miles that lay between her and the town of Soldotna offered plenty of time for reflection. Travel time was a blessing and offered the solitude she needed between cases.

A reminding nose nudged her mittened hand.

Christa laughed and patted her beautifully marked Alaskan malamute. "Sorry, Aurora. With God and you, I'm never alone." She opened the driver's door. "In, girl." Aurora barked, leaped into the Explorer, and crossed to the "copilot" seat. She looked at her owner as if to say, "C'mon, slowpoke. What are we waiting for?"

Christa slid behind the wheel. Closing the door and fastening her seat belt, she accused, "You're a faker. Before we're halfway to Soldotna, you'll be curled up and asleep, with that gorgeous tail of yours covering your nose, as usual."

Aurora cocked her head, looking as though she were smiling. Blue eyes that matched Christa's in color but were considered a disqualifying fault by the AKC — the

American Kennel Club — suggested near-human intelligence. She sat back on her haunches and relaxed. A week in a kennel had obviously not been to her liking.

"My sentiments exactly." Christa started the engine and put the Explorer into gear. "It's good to be off that last case. Why I ever agreed to care for a pampered, wealthy woman is beyond me. She must never have heard of the Emancipation Proclamation. She treated me more like a slave than a professional. Imagine, refusing to let a nice dog like you on her property. As if you'd hurt her precious yard or flowers." Christa felt an unrepentant grin form. "She doesn't have any flowers now. What few escaped frostbite became a late-night snack for a roving moose. Good thing I like the critters. They are all over the place up here."

Christa sighed with contentment. "No unpleasant, cloying atmosphere for us today, Aurora. Just fresh air and people who appreciate my services."

A sharp bark brought a rise in Christa's already-high spirits. "Okay, our services. You're part of this team, except when I have fussbudget patients." She ruffled Aurora's thick fur. How many times had she taken her medical skills on the road in the past two years? When she added helicopter calls to remote areas beyond her trusty four-wheel-drive SUV's capabilities, the total was staggering.

Happiness rode with Christa and Aurora on this day of days. Having faced and conquered a multitude of obstacles, they were well prepared with food, blankets, medical supplies, cell phone, and extra batteries. Christa's course in minor vehicle repair, her nurse's and nurse-practitioner's training, and a supply of common sense, were supplemented by an unwavering faith in the God she met as a child and had worshiped ever since.

"Aurora, if anyone had told me two years ago I'd be here with you . . ."

A loud snore showed that her copilot had succumbed to sleep, leaving Christa to again reflect on how blessed she really was. For the second time that morning, she prayed, *Thank You, God. If it weren't for Susan . . .* This time she mentally drifted into the past, although eyes and hands remained alert to her present surroundings. . . .

Susan. Flaxen-haired with laughing eyes the unusual blue found only in the heart of a glacier. Susan. Three inches shorter and fifteen pounds lighter than Christa's graceful five-feet-eight-inch height and 140 pounds. Susan, who adored her big sister and was dearly loved in return. Christa laughed in pure delight. One of her favorite memories of her sister was the day she pouted and demanded, "How come I couldn't be adopted like Christa? You picked her, but you just had me. You couldn't send me back."

Ron Bishop had laughed. "You were both miracles, Susan. You know the story."

A look of wonder replaced Susan's pout, and words tumbled out. "You and Mommy thought I'd never come. When Christa was born and her mommy died, you took care of Christa 'cause her daddy was sick. He never got better, so you kept Christa."

"That's right," Leigh Bishop said. "We believe God sent us to help Mr. Jensen and gave Christa to us. Her daddy wanted her to have his name as well as ours —"

"That's why she's Christa Jensen Bishop," Susan interrupted. She clapped her hands, her face wreathed in smiles. "And when she was two, God sent another miracle. Me." She had beamed at them all. "Christa was really, really happy to have a little sister!"

I still am, Christa thought, her gaze intent on the highway. There was always the danger of animals straying onto the road. *Thank You, God, for two sets of wonderful parents, even though I only know my birth mother and father through the Bishops.* A kaleidoscope of memories swirled through her mind: school; church; the good smell of leather in the Bishops' sporting goods store; the two-story home on Queen Anne Hill, furnished with love and good taste rather than an abundance of money. College and training to fulfill Christa's dream of becoming first a nurse, then a nurse-practitioner. Susan had chosen to attend business college and became an administrative assistant at the Seattle Veterans' Hospital, but all she really wanted was to marry a good man and raise happy, healthy children.

"What about your childhood dream of being a missionary?" Christa teased.

"There are probably just as many or more heathens right here in Seattle. I'll be a home-front missionary," was Susan's saucy reply, typical of the happy-go-lucky personality that sometimes hid the depth of her love for God. Her devotion equaled Christa's and bonded them in a sisterhood of friendship so strong it even prevented Christa from laughing at some of Susan's wild schemes. Like writing jingles and entering "Complete this sentence in twenty-five words or less and win the vacation (or furniture, or wardrobe) of your dreams" contests!

Susan met "Mr. Right" just after her twenty-second birthday. She confessed to Christa, who was too busy with her career to allow herself to fall in love, "It's everything they say. Stars in your eyes. Walking on clouds. Waiting for the phone to ring." She hugged her sister fiercely. "But we'll never let anything come between us. You'll always be there for me if I need you, won't you?"

"Of course." Yet even as she promised, Christa had the strange feeling all was not well. It proved true. "Mr. Right" dumped Susan a few weeks later. On a day when the heavens had opened and rivers of rain poured down on the city, his engagement announcement to a former girlfriend appeared in the *Seattle Times*.

"I can take being jilted," Susan spat out. "But to have someone I trusted do it this way is rotten." Her eyes flashed blue fire. "I'm just glad to know what he's really like!" She raised her chin. "It *would* happen on a day like today. What's that old poem?" She ran to a nearby bookcase and snatched up a worn poetry book. "Here it is. 'The Rainy Day,' by Henry Wadsworth Longfellow. Wadsworth. What a name!"

Christa gave a sigh of relief. Susan's pride was more hurt than her heart, or she wouldn't be able to sound so normal. "Read it aloud."

"Okay." Susan deepened her voice to fit the contents of the quotation.

" 'The day is cold, and dark, and dreary;
It rains, and the wind is never weary;
The vine still clings to the moldering wall,
But at every gust the dead leaves fall,
And the day is dark and dreary.

'My life is cold, and dark, and dreary;
It rains, and the wind is never weary;
My thoughts still cling to the moldering
    Past,
But the hopes of youth fall thick in the blast
And the days are dark and dreary.' "

Susan tossed the book down. "Rats! I'd forgotten how mournful this is! If it doesn't get better, I'm outta here." She made a face, grabbed the book, and read in a voice that softened with each line:

" 'Be still, sad heart! and cease repining;
Behind the clouds is the sun still shining;
Thy fate is the common fate of all,
Into each life some rain must fall,
Some days must be dark and dreary.' "

For a long time, neither spoke. Then

Susan shrugged. "If you subscribe to the misery-loves-company theory, I guess this helps. Look, the rain's stopping. Let's go for a walk." How like her! Impulsive, yet with flashes of wisdom that often made Christa marvel.

Susan made no more mention of "Mr. Right." Then one day, she danced into the blue and white dining room where Christa and their parents were already at the dinner table. Her soft green dress made her look like a wood sprite in spring. "Guess what!"

Christa's heart leaped to her throat. *Please, God, don't let her say Mr. Right-Turned-Wrong broke his engagement and wants her back.*

Susan didn't wait for an answer. She said in a mysterious voice, "Big sister, remember when you said you'd always be there for me? Now's your chance. Pack your clothes. Tell Mom and Dad good-bye. We're going to Alaska."

"We're what?"

"You are what?" her parents had chorused.

A brilliant smile spread across Susan's animated face. "Christa and I are going to Alaska. I told you entering all those contests would pay off."

Ron Bishop just stared. Leigh gasped. "You actually won?"

Susan smirked. "Trust me. I won an all-expenses-paid cruise for two. The contest was sponsored by a new travel agency that just opened up downtown. The promotion was a way to attract customers. All you had to do was stop by and write where you wanted to go to get away from it all and why in twenty-five words or less. So I did."

Her father chuckled and looked curious. "What did you write?"

Susan's pink and white complexion darkened until she had looked like a full-blown rose. "It's kind of embarrassing."

"Susan Bishop, exactly what did you say?" Leigh demanded.

"Uh, I was still in a bad mood over the engagement, so I wrote, 'I want to cruise to Alaska. My boyfriend dumped me. There are more men than women in the Last Frontier. Maybe I'll meet "Mr. Right." ' Exactly twenty-five words."

Ron Bishop had tilted his chair back and roared. Leigh stared at her daughter, appalled. Christa blurted out, "Are you mad? Contests publish winning essays, if you can call them that. Everyone in Seattle is going to know what you wrote!"

Susan's eyes widened; then she shrugged. "Who cares? We're going to see the land of the midnight sun, aurora borealis, whales, and icebergs. You'll go, won't you?"

"Traveling with you may be taking my life in my hands," Christa said. "But of course I'll go."

A few weeks later, she and Susan left Seattle behind and began their journey. To their dismay, instead of sailing up the Inside Passage as expected, they headed out to sea — and into a storm. Susan didn't feel well, so she took a pill and went to bed.

Christa felt fine physically but was terrified. She'd always been afraid of water; now she lay trying to sleep in a bed that felt like a bucking bronco. *What am I doing here, Lord?* she prayed. *I am so scared. Please give me peace.* She closed her eyes. A picture formed: Jesus, walking on the troubled waters of the Sea of Galilee. "This would be a good place for You to walk," she whispered. Some of her nervousness subsided. For the next hour or so, she drowsed; then another roll of the ship brought a fresh wave of fear. "Are you still out there?" she asked, glad God had a sense of humor.

The next morning had brought gray skies, but by the time they reached Juneau, the day was glorious. So was the rest of the cruise. Both Susan and Christa fell wholeheartedly, unreservedly in love with Alaska.

Shortly after their return, Susan announced she was applying for a job at the VA hospital in Anchorage. "Dad and Mom are talking about taking a year off and traveling," she said. "Home won't be home without them. I hear Alaska calling, and your nursing skills are in demand everywhere. This may be our last chance to strike out on our own before we marry and settle down, Christa. Will you come with me?" She grinned. "Who knows? We may even be swept off our feet by a couple of strong Alaskan men!"

Christa couldn't deny the prospect tantalized her. After intense prayer, she agreed to go, hoping Susan was right when she said they wouldn't regret it.

Susan was *right.* Three days after reaching Anchorage, Christa met Major Gavin Scott, a pilot in the U.S. Air Force.

CHAPTER 3

Gavin. The mere thought of her fiancé sent joy flowing through Christa like warm honey. "Please, God, keep him safe and bring him home," she murmured. Aurora stirred, licked Christa's hand, then settled back into sleep, leaving her mistress to relive the weeks and months after she met the tall, dark-haired pilot. Once more her present surroundings melted into a montage of memories, beginning with the moment she and Susan reached Anchorage and first saw their new home away from home. . . .

"This can't be where we're going to live," Susan had exclaimed. Her eyes opened so wide, they looked like twin aquamarines. "It's a fairy-tale cottage!"

"Try your keys," their taxi driver remarked. "If they fit, this is the place!" He guffawed.

Christa laughed. "You're right about that." With Susan at her heels, she walked up the stepping-stone pathway that divided the lawn into two plush green carpets bordered by flowers. Tall evergreens on both sides of the small white house with dark green roof, shutters, and front door promised privacy from their neighbors.

"Hurry, Christa," Susan ordered.

Heart pounding, fingers trembling, Christa crossed the covered porch with its white wicker chairs and table. Before she could insert the key in the lock, the door swung inward. A robust, pleasant-faced woman in denim shirt and jeans appeared — along with a sweet and spicy fragrance that reminded Christa she hadn't had lunch.

Susan's gasp of disappointment echoed her sister's sense of loss, but Christa managed to stammer, "I–I'm terribly sorry. We must have the wrong house."

The woman chuckled. "Not if you're the Bishop sisters. Welcome to Anchorage. I'm Molly Hunter. I live next door. The Hagensons said you'd be here today, so I brought over an apple pie. My, but they're glad to know you'll be taking care of their home while —"

"Hey, ladies, the meter's running," the taxi driver called. "You can flap your jaws after we unload your luggage."

Well, Christa thought, *there are colorful*

characters in Alaska, too.

After the taxi disappeared down the quiet, tree-lined street, Molly led the way inside. "Like I was saying, the Hagensons feel you two are an answer to prayer."

"We're the ones who believe that," Susan burst out. "We were worried we couldn't afford a nice place. Then a church friend said he knew a couple who had volunteered for an overseas humanitarian mission that would last a year or two." She shook her head. "We still don't feel it's right that the Hagensons only want us to pay the utilities and for any repairs that might be necessary."

Molly shook her head. "Don't let that bother you. If God hadn't sent you, the Hagensons would have had to hire a house sitter. Don't worry about repairs, either. The place is in excellent shape. Besides, my husband is real handy and enjoys helping folks." She glanced at her watch. "I need to be running along, but would you like to go to church with Richard and me this Sunday? It's a real Bible-based church and not far away. You can have dinner with us afterward."

"We would love to," Christa said from a full heart. She voiced her thoughts to Susan after Molly left. "Any doubts we may have had about coming here are certainly dwindling," she said. "God is so good. A story-book cottage and a couple of earthly angels for neighbors! What more could we want?"

Susan grinned. "Just two strong Alaskan men to sweep us off our feet."

"You're hopeless," Christa told her. "Now, let's dive into that apple pie, then check out our new home." She led the way to the cheerful kitchen — and discovered well-stocked cupboards, refrigerator, and freezer, courtesy of the Hunters.

Sunday morning dawned bright, clear, and cold. Christa and Susan decided to walk to church and meet the Hunters there. They started early so they could enjoy the residential neighborhood in which they now lived, giving a moose — which showed no signs of yielding the right-of-way — a wide berth. They arrived at church rosy-cheeked and excited. "Look!" Susan clutched her sister's arm. "There's another moose!"

"Where?" Christa turned her head to see. *Thud.* The next moment, she was sitting on the sidewalk feeling stupid and staring up into a pair of concerned gray eyes. It didn't help to hear Susan giggling behind her.

A strong, uniformed arm reached down and helped her to her feet. "Are you hurt? I am so sorry."

Susan giggled louder.

Christa was torn between wanting to squash her sister and answer honestly. She rubbed one elbow. "The only thing hurt is my dignity." Suddenly the humor of the situation hit her. The tall, dark-haired man she had plowed into while moose-gazing could have stepped from an Air Force recruiting ad. In spite of his recent impact with a mortified nurse-practitioner, there wasn't a wrinkle in his perfect-fitting uniform. Sunlight turned the wings — indicating he was a pilot — to gleaming silver.

"I'm Gavin Scott," her victim said. "Glad to hear the damage is minimal." His eyes twinkled and his mouth twitched. "Do I dare say 'nice running into you'?"

"Not unless you intend to beat a strategic retreat. I'm Christa Jensen Bishop. It's nice to meet you." She cast a withering glance at her companion. "This is my sister, Susan, although right now I'm not sure I want to claim her."

"Is this your first time at our church?" he asked with a nod toward Susan.

"Yes." Christa liked the way he said "our church." It made her feel welcome, at home. It also established a rapport with the handsome officer.

"Oh, here you are." Molly Hunter bustled

up. "Have you met Gavin?"

"Yes," Susan demurely said. "He has been most helpful, hasn't he, Christa?"

Molly evidently didn't catch the undertones in the seemingly innocent remark. "Christa and Susan are my new neighbors, now that the Hagensons are gone. Christa is a nurse-practitioner and will be on the road a lot. Susan has a job at the veterans' hospital. By the way, Gavin, what about coming for dinner, since your folks are out of town for a few days? The girls will be there."

Gavin raised one dark eyebrow. "If it's all right with them," he politely said.

Major, you'll never know just how all right it is. Appalled at the thought, Christa hesitated a split second before answering, just long enough for doubt to darken Gavin's watching eyes and rob them of the fun that had sparkled in their depths.

Susan, who could always read her sister like an open magazine, more than made up for Christa's lapse in manners. "We would both be delighted," she said firmly.

"Good." Molly shepherded her little flock up the steps and through the church door. "Richard's already inside. We can all sit together."

Susan Bishop had the cunning of Machiavelli when it came to furthering her schemes. Christa had to admire the way she maneuvered the five of them into the pew so that Susan ended up on the far side of the Hunters with Gavin in the center aisle seat next to Christa. He didn't seem to mind. They shared a hymnal, and his rich, deep voice blended with her softer one. At several points in the service, Gavin glanced down at her and smiled, as if expressing agreement with what the minister was saying.

That Sunday had been just the beginning. When their limited free time coincided, Gavin showed Christa the many faces of Alaska. Susan and whatever young man she happened to fancy at the time accompanied them. The bonds of friendship ripened. With the future uncertain, it was enough to experience the simple joy of being together.

One particularly memorable excursion began on a day all blue and green, white and gold. Gavin had arranged a surprise for the sisters. "Wear layers of clothing," he advised. "It can be both cold and warm — and where we are going is one of the most beautiful, historical places in Alaska." His smile made Christa's heart soar like the eagles she watched gliding in the sky. "We're off to Skagway, which means 'Home of the North Wind,' to take the White Pass and Yukon Route. It was built in 1898 during the Klondike Gold Rush and is something you'll never forget."

Though familiar with the rugged mountains of Washington State, Christa and Susan had never seen such grandeur. The narrow-gauge railway hugged slopes on its ten-foot-wide roadbed blasted out of sheer rock, a feat said to be impossible. Waterfalls and streams cascaded from towering glaciers thousands of feet to the bottom of Dead Horse Gulch, where the bleached bones of pack animals, driven to their deaths by those in search of gold, remained. The train chugged through a 250-foot tunnel, midnight-black and scary.

Yet of everything they had seen, one thing stood out: a grim reminder that the evil in the hearts of men never ceases. Christa would never forget the look on Gavin's face when he pointed out the remains of a huge wooden trestle. "There was a great deal of fear during World War II that the Japanese might invade Alaska. Military personnel guarded the trestle twenty-four hours a day. In spite of their vigilance, a bomb was found at its base. Thank God it was unexploded." His lips set in a grim line. "The saboteur was never found."

"The same sort of thing is going on today," Susan blazed. Great tears dimmed her eyes. "Blowing up bridges is bad enough, but what is happening now is worse. People all over the world are being killed by those who are taught it is honorable and glorious to murder the innocent." She buried her face in her hands.

Christa clutched her sister's hand, too moved to speak.

Gavin laid one hand over hers. "I pray for the day when bloodshed will cease. Until then, I am called to fight evil wherever it is found. Dad and Mom raised me to believe in God, family, and country. I'll do whatever Uncle Sam asks of me."

A blanket of dread descended on Christa. There was something in his voice . . .

"Gavin, have you received new orders?" she whispered, hating her inability to keep her voice from shaking.

"Yes. I've been fortunate enough to have been stationed at Elmendorf until now, but it's been decided I'm needed elsewhere."

Christa's throat dried. "Do you know where?" How could she stand for him to go away? She hadn't realized how much she would miss him until the threat of his leaving surfaced. Winter loomed and Anchorage would be bleak without him.

Gavin shook his head. An expression of regret and something more flickered in his somber eyes. Something that quickened Christa's heartbeat, even though she felt she was being suffocated with fear. "Destination unknown at this point. It's going to be hard to go." He tightened his grip on her hand, then gently released it. "Let's talk about something pleasant — like getting the best ice cream cones in Skagway."

Christa hadn't been able to speak, but Susan valiantly rose to the occasion. She freed her hand, dug in her jacket pocket for a tissue, and blew her nose. "Sounds good to me."

"Great. I know a place downtown where . . ."

Aurora roused and gave a short bark. Christa's thoughts returned to the present. "Smart dog, always waking up just before we get to our patient. Now to find him." The medical group for which she worked always obtained directions. Following them often wasn't easy! However, today Christa drove straight to the home of a stubborn old man she had attended after he suffered a heart attack while visiting a friend who lived in the mountains near Anchorage.

Christa had been caring for a sick family nearby.

The man's heart was simply worn out. When he learned his condition, he said, "Well, the Good Lord's kept it ticking for almost ninety years. Can I go home?"

"Yes, with medicine and a nurse to visit you. Who is your doctor?"

He cackled. "Ain't got one. Don't want a nurse, either, unless it's you."

Christa grinned. "If you'll agree to let me contact someone in Soldotna to look after you for a few days, I'll come as soon as I can. Okay if I bring my dog?"

He frowned. "It ain't some itty-bitty, ratty critter, is it? Can't stand 'em."

"Neither can I," she confessed. "Aurora is an Alaskan malamute."

"Okay. You and A-Roarer come soon." He cackled again. "Don't wait too long."

Christa didn't. As soon as she got back to home base, she arranged to spend a few days with the man, hoping she might talk him into accepting help from a local nurse.

Now she pulled into the yard of a modest house, noting with satisfaction the lazy drift of smoke curling from the chimney. "Come on, 'A-Roarer.' Time to go to work."

Chapter 4

The Middle East

Of all the instructions given to Gavin Scott, Ben Sharp, and their fellow pilots before they were allowed to go on reconnaissance missions, nothing was stressed as much or as often as what to do in case of emergencies. Gavin would never forget his introduction to the hard-bitten officer in charge of orientation. He drilled procedure into the fliers' heads with the zeal of a dedicated Sunday school teacher implanting the Ten Commandments in his students' brains.

"First, remember that the EF-111's ejection capsule has an automatic distress beacon," he said. "The bad guys will hear it just like we will. When you hit dirt, grab your survival gear and run as if your life depends on it. It may." He paused to let the warning sink in. "Activate your personal radios and wait for the choppers to call."

Gavin felt ice worms crawl up and down

155

his spine. The fear of coming down in the wilds of Alaska had never affected him like this. He squared his shoulders, knowing that every word of the lecture was being indelibly branded on his very soul.

"God forbid any of you will ever be forced down," the instructor fervently said. "In the event it happens, follow procedure — to the letter. Do not, I repeat, *do not* stay with your aircraft. Get to the nearest cover, if you have to crawl on hands and knees. Or on your belly! Once there, don't budge until help comes."

A wintry smile briefly lightened his hatchet face. "Help will come. Our helicopter crews make bloodhounds look like amateurs when it comes to rescuing our own." His smile faded into a steely gaze that traveled from face to face. It left Gavin feeling he had been stripped and searched. "Any questions?"

Paralyzing silence followed.

"Very well. Dismissed." The officer saluted and strode quickly away from the training area.

Gavin turned to Ben. His friend looked like Gavin felt — as if they'd just survived an enemy attack. Ben's brown eyes had darkened to almost black. "He made things pretty clear, didn't he?" Gavin asked.

"Yeah. That's good, though. It should discourage anyone dumb enough to try hot-dogging." Ben lowered his voice. "I just pray we never have to use the information."

"So do I."

Now it was time. Time to put into practice what they had been taught. Time to survive by following the procedures they had reviewed again and again during the months they had been flying overseas. After the first stunned moment when Gavin confessed he couldn't see, Ben took command.

"We could be a lot worse off," he pointed out. "I can see. You can help support me. We'll make it."

Gavin responded to the studied cheerfulness in his RSO's voice. "Of course. Between us we have everything we need — three good legs; two good eyes. Let's get out of here."

"Sure, as soon as I gather up stuff to take care of that head of yours. These limestone hills and sand dunes don't offer much in the way of hospitals and clinics!"

They don't offer much in the way of cover, either. Gavin bit down hard on the thought. Not being able to see their surroundings left his imagination wide open. He could picture unfriendly eyes watching them from behind the hills and dunes Ben had mentioned. *Stop it,* he silently ordered himself. *That kind of thinking is dangerous.*

God, we need You. I need You. Panic is not an option. Neither is fear. Are You there?

Encouragement came to mind and soothed him like a glass of ice water on a scorching day. Psalm 46:1: *"God is our refuge and strength, a very present help in trouble."* It was closely followed by Psalm 121:1–2: *"I will lift up mine eyes unto the hills, from whence cometh my help. My help cometh from the Lord, which made heaven and earth."*

Despite his heaviness of heart, Gavin grinned. He'd always associated the scripture with his beloved Alaskan mountains. Yet the God of towering peaks was the God of limestone hills. He was just as able to protect His children from danger lurking behind them as from the ravening Alaskan wolves that traveled in packs and wreaked havoc.

"Ready?"

Gavin ignored his throbbing head. "Ready, Burgess Benjamin."

"Did you or did you not put me in charge of this little expedition?" Ben demanded.

Gavin fought his pain. "I did."

"Then that temporarily makes me your superior. Let's have a little respect."

It was too much effort to think up a suitable reply. Besides, Gavin knew he'd need every ounce of energy he possessed to make it to cover.

"This little hike is going to test us as we've never before been tested," Ben warned. "It would be harrowing under normal circumstances. Now . . ."

" 'By the grace of God and a lot of grit,' as Dad used to say, 'we'll do it.' " Gavin didn't add the obvious. They had to — for each other's sake even more than their own.

"You've got that right. Here. Give me your right arm. It's my left leg that's busted up. We'll do our own version of a three-legged race."

Wounded and in pain, they started their journey. The distance that lay between them and cover loomed endlessly in their minds. The best they could do was plod. Sheer willpower kept them going. With each painful step, Ben leaned harder on Gavin, who could hear his friend's harsh breathing from the effort. Then Ben staggered and crumpled to the ground, pulling Gavin with him.

Gavin rolled away from his friend. "This isn't working. I'll carry you."

For once Ben didn't argue. "You're going to have to, at least until this crazy leg of mine is rested. I'll navigate."

"More like playing guide dog," Gavin said as he hoisted his friend into a fireman's carry position. "Concentrate on what's just ahead. It will only take one hummock to fell us. If I go down again, I don't know if I'll be able to get up and continue."

Step by shuffling step, they crossed the unfriendly land. The loss of blood from Gavin's head wound steadily took its toll on his considerable strength. So did Ben's weight. He lost track of time and place. All he could think of was putting one foot in front of the other. Left. Right. Left. Right. Strange. When had he deserted the Air Force and become part of the infantry? Left. Right. Left. Right. Would the march never cease? Where were they going? Why? It was hot. So hot.

Something warm and wet slid down his face. The next instant, he tasted blood.

It brought him to his senses. He stumbled, regained his balance, and said, "I'm bleeding again, Ben. Better put another compress on the wound."

"It's time to stop and rest anyway," Ben said. "We won't go on until we get the bleeding under control."

"Good." Gavin slid to the ground. "I'll catch a few z's, and —"

"No!" Ben grabbed him by the shoulders and forced him to sit up. "You know the drill. No sleeping when you have a head wound."

Gavin knew he was right. He had to keep going, no matter how slowly.

When Gavin's wound stopped seeping, he wearily got to his feet. Ben insisted on walking as much as he could, which helped. Two lone souls in a country far from home — both desperately prayed that their strength would hold out long enough for them to travel the remaining distance to a safe place.

Hours that felt like centuries later, Gavin and Ben found cover. Now all they could do was wait and pray, knowing full well the danger wasn't over. God grant that help would come before they were discovered by unfriendly forces and taken captive — or worse.

Gradually they relaxed, although they didn't let down their vigilance against possible threat. Gavin's mind cleared. He told Ben, who never tired of hearing about Alaska, more stories. They talked of home. Of Christa. And of why they were there, far away from those they loved.

"If I had to put it in a few words, it would be something Christa said shortly after we met," Gavin flatly stated. He struggled to recall her exact words and the way she looked during their conversation. "Something really special happened when she and her sister, Susan, were on their Alaskan cruise, and —"

"I hope Susan is still single when we get back to America," Ben interrupted. "She sounds like my kind of woman. What are the chances of an invite to Anchorage?"

Gavin laughed, the first time since they started their arduous journey. "You're welcome anytime. You might be just what Susan needs. She's been playing the field ever since she got to Alaska. I have the feeling she just may not have met the right guy yet." He laughed again, even though it made his head hurt. "If Christa had already been taken, I'd be pitching a tent at Susan's doorstep! By the way, both of the sisters are strong Christians."

"They sound like keepers," Ben said. After a long moment, he ran a grimy hand over his matted curls and added, "I hope she goes for redheads! In the meantime, what were you saying about their cruise?"

"The dinner stewards and room attendants came from all over the world. They represented more than fifty countries, many of them under the rule of cruel dictators. Christa said the young men reminded her of little boys, homesick for their families. They were so eager and appreciative of the chance to talk with Americans! Many expressed how people in their homelands loved America and what we are doing for them."

Ben grunted. "Different from what you hear in the media, huh?"

"Right. It was also interesting to hear what the ship's employees had to say about the way they were treated. They love having American tourists because most are friendly. They take time to visit, to ask those who serve them if they have wives and kids, and so on. Evidently it isn't that way with everyone." Gavin sighed.

"One morning after Susan left the dining room, Christa lingered to finish a conversation with a young man from a South American country. He confirmed what others had said: Many European tourists are much more formal. They consider the stewards and room attendants servants and ignore them as human beings.

" 'How does that make you feel?' Christa said. 'I'd hate being treated that way.'

"The young man sadly shook his head. 'Only in America can you be somebody.'

"Christa could barely hold back the tears until she got out of the dining room. It reminded her how important it is for America to help those who are oppressed, whether by cruel rulers or caste systems. It also shows that millions of people around the world still appreciate us and the God-given freedom we want to share — even when it sometimes means giving our lives to help others."

"Like Christ gave His life to free us from sin," Ben said. "Bringing light into a lost, dark world."

"Yes." Something he needed to tell Ben hovered on the edge of Gavin's consciousness. Something to do with the darkness in which he was now trapped. There. He had it.

"Before help comes, I need to tell you something. From the time I was a kid, I knew what to do if I got lost. Find the North Star and take my bearings from it. If clouds covered the sky and I couldn't see the North Star, I should ask God what to do." He cleared his throat. "I can't see the North Star or anything else, Ben. The future looks black. Unless my sight returns on its own, this 'white hawk' is grounded. Even if surgery restores my vision, I can never fly for the Air Force again. It's policy."

"I know."

Gavin knew the pain in Ben's voice did

not come from his injuries. Before he could respond, a welcome noise sounded in his ears: the *whup-whup* of a rescue helicopter, sweeter to the downed fliers' ears than the swish of angels' wings.

Exhausted by the ordeal, Gavin let himself relax. His last conscious memory was of lifting off, accompanied by Ben's taunt to the crew.

"What took you so long? Where have you been? Out chasing camels?"

CHAPTER 5

An Air Force hospital in Texas

"Hang in there, Major. We're going to take care of you."

The voice with a hint of Southern drawl penetrated the murk that clouded Gavin Scott's brain. Where was he? He tried to turn toward the unknown speaker, but his body felt like someone had clamped it in a vise. Too weary to figure it out, Gavin drifted into a never-never land somewhere between consciousness and reality. . . .

Scene after sunlit scene replayed in his tired mind, elusive as a dancing butterfly hovering over a hillside adorned by fireweed. Its hue was no brighter than the face of the young woman laughing at him from behind a great armful of rose purple flowers. It was Christa Jensen Bishop, who had fallen at his feet while moose-gazing.

It was so good to be back in Alaska! Back in the country he loved, with the woman he believed God had chosen as a mate for the "white hawk." For years Gavin had strived to become worthy of the love of a good woman. If or when God sent someone to Gavin, he would devote his life to being a godly husband and father.

He basked in the warmth of Christa's smile, a smile that remained as steady and true as the first time he had seen her. Gavin had never discounted love at first sight but believed people needed to take a second look before jumping into a commitment. Yet during their short time together, Gavin became convinced he and Christa were meant to spend the rest of their lives together. The wistful look in her blue eyes shouted that she was learning to care for him.

Gavin said nothing to Christa of his growing love. "It wouldn't be fair," he told his father one night when the aurora borealis put on a show worthy of a standing ovation.

"Why not? Will it be any easier if you go without telling her?" Mac Scott grunted and placed a strong hand on his son's shoulder. "I felt the same until your mother said she loved me and asked me what I was going to do about it!" He fell silent. "I married her and let her traipse along with me whenever possible."

Gavin's heartbeat quickened at the prospect of having Christa with him, but he shook his head. "It's too soon. Marriage isn't an option right now."

Mac's grip tightened. "So who said anything about marriage? You can at least get engaged." He pointed at the dancing lights in the sky. "Go buy your girl a ring with a stone that shoots sparkles like that. It will give her something to hang on to while you're away."

Gavin turned to face his father. "And if I don't come back?"

"Then you and she will at least have had the joy of today." With a convulsive grip of his son's shoulder, Mac marched away, leaving Gavin to ponder.

The next day he enlisted Susan Bishop's help in choosing a diamond ring that made her eyes widen. "It's perfect," she exclaimed, holding it up to the light. The full spectrum of colors shone from the depths of the clear white stone. "If Christa doesn't want it, I'll take it," she roguishly added. "Well, not really. I'm not ready to settle down." She moved the ring back and forth. "This reminds me of Christa's and my cruise. One night just before midnight, she looked out our window to say good night to the ocean. 'Quick, come and see,' she called. 'Hurry!'

"I ran to the window. Shimmering golden light filled the sky above the snowcapped mountains. We threw sweats and parkas over our night wear and raced up to the top deck. It was windy and freezing cold, but for the next fifteen minutes, we saw the northern lights. They weren't colored like the ones here but white and gorgeous." Susan blinked. "Neither of us will ever forget it."

Gavin's heart warmed to her appreciation of beauty. "I never had a sister," he told her. "But if Christa says yes, I will."

Susan's eyes glistened. "She'd better say yes. As has been said before, a good man is hard to find." She sighed. "Trust me. I know."

She sounded so sad, it made Gavin wonder, *Was there a lost love in Susan's past?* If so, it would explain why she never dated even the most charming, persistent suitor more than a few times before switching to someone else.

The night before Gavin left Anchorage, he picked up Christa and drove to a spot where they could see Cook Inlet, the frosted white mountains, and the city. "Are you dressed warm enough for a short walk?" he asked.

"Toasty." She snuggled deeper into her

scarlet parka and pulled the hood up. "Where are we going?"

"Not far." Gavin led her to a huge rock nearby. All the pretty speeches he'd secretly practiced deserted him. He took both her mittened hands and looked deep into her moonlit face. "I love you, Christa. I always will. If God brings me safely home from wherever I'm sent, will you marry me?"

Her eyes filled with tears. She slipped from his grasp and stepped back.

Gavin's spirits plummeted to earth like a paratrooper whose parachute had failed to open. *Dad was wrong,* he thought. *It's too soon.*

The next moment, she clasped her mittened hands in front of her. "I love you, Gavin. I'll marry you anytime, anywhere you say."

When her answer sank in, Gavin felt like the white hawk for which he was named — the white hawk that soared to great heights. A beloved psalm sang in his heart: *"When I consider thy heavens, the work of thy fingers, the moon and the stars, which thou hast ordained; what is man, that thou art mindful of him? . . . [Thou] hast crowned him with glory and honour."*

The final words fit the wondrous night as no others could have done. Gavin pulled

Christa close. His silent prayer ascended to the heavens. *Thank You, Lord. May our lives always bring You glory.*

For a time it was enough to simply hold Christa. Her head rested just above his heart. Could she hear its quickened cadence? The love that coursed through him with every beat? Yes, for her arms slid around his waist and her face turned toward his as a sunflower turns toward the sun.

"Is it real, Gavin?" she whispered. "Or is it all a dream? Will I wake up back in Seattle, never having come to Alaska, never having met you? I couldn't bear it."

His blood raced. He laughed so loudly, it seemed the heavens rang. "It's real, sweetheart." He freed one hand and took a small, velvet-covered case from his pocket. Unwilling to release her, he unsuccessfully struggled with one hand to open the case. "Here. You do it."

Christa laughed and took off her mittens. The case popped open. The diamond glittered bright as the twinkling stars above. "It–it's beautiful. So pure."

"It reminds me of you." Gavin reluctantly loosed her from his encircling arms, slipped the ring on her finger, and kissed it. "Someday we will stand in church and take our marriage vows before God, our family, and our friends. I look forward to seeing you walk down the aisle in your wedding dress and knowing you are mine. But I don't want to wait that long to exchange vows. Christa Jensen Bishop, I promise you here and now: I will love and cherish you. I will guard your happiness with all that is within me, as long as we both shall live."

With a little cry that Gavin knew came from joy, she flew back into his embrace like a homing pigeon.

"Wake up, Major. It's all over."

Christa vanished. The night did not, except neither moon nor stars pierced the darkness surrounding Gavin. He struggled to understand. After what felt like centuries, he managed to croak, "What's all over?"

"The surgery on your eyes. We got you back to the good ol' U.S.A. posthaste after you went down in the Middle East, so you could get the finest medical help possible. We take care of our own."

Where had he heard that before? Gavin wondered. Oh, yes, the instructor who gave preflight instructions on emergency procedures. "Help will come. Our helicopter crews make bloodhounds look like amateurs when it comes to rescuing our own."

Gavin involuntarily raised his hand.

"Don't touch your head!"

Memory of the disaster returned in a rush. The fire. His futile attempts to extinguish it. Ejecting from the Raven. The endless trek to cover. Ben's forcing him to stay awake when all Gavin wanted to do was lie down and sleep, hoping that when he awakened, it would turn out to have been a nightmare. And finally, the sweet *whup-whup* sound that announced help had come, with Ben mouthing off to the helicopter crew about taking so long to get there.

"Captain Sharp?" Gavin hoarsely asked.

"He's fine. Some torn ligaments will keep him grounded for a while, but he'll be good as new in time. So will you, Major. There's every indication the surgery was a complete success and your sight will be normal."

Normal? When, as far as the U.S. Air Force was concerned, he was a has-been? Ben would heal and fly reconnaissance again. Major Gavin Scott would — what? Well, at least they would be home for Thanksgiving and Christmas, as Ben had hoped.

No use thinking about it now. He had the rest of his life to figure out why God had allowed this to happen. Or more accurately, why He hadn't prevented it. God didn't cause aircraft fires, but why hadn't He protected the men who served Him? Why hadn't He healed Gavin's eyes spontaneously so surgery wouldn't have been necessary?

God, this is more than I can bear. You know my dream of following in Dad's footsteps. It began the first time he strapped me into the seat of a plane.

Suddenly Gavin wanted to go home. Home to Mom and Dad, to everything he knew and loved. Most of all, to Christa. He clung to the thought while waiting to be cleared to return to Alaska. Yet troubled minds and hurting souls offer fertile soil for seeds of doubt. So it was with Gavin. The girl he left behind had fallen in love with a dashing pilot who soared far above the earth. How would she respond to a fallen "white hawk"?

Gavin fell into a deep depression. Did he have the right to hold Christa to a promise made under far different circumstances? Again and again he told himself, "Don't jump to conclusions. Christa is true. Christa is loyal. She will stick by her man."

Unfortunately, those very traits magnified the problem in Gavin's worried mind and brought a dozen more. Perhaps he and Christa had been so caught up in the danger that went with Gavin's job, they had convinced themselves the love they shared was God's will. What if He was trying to show them they had been mistaken? Even though Gavin knew such misgivings were normal under the circumstances, they fed on his weakened condition and haunted him more each day.

The emotional battle inevitably took its toll. Gavin worked himself into such a state that he developed a fever. "What have you been doing to yourself?" the physician in charge barked. "You should have been out of here by now and on your way home."

"I don't want to go home." Gavin was appalled at his terse reply. When had dread of returning to Anchorage begun gnawing at him like a husky with a bone? What did it matter? The statement was true, although he hadn't realized it until he spoke.

Shaggy brows beetled over the doctor's keen eyes. "Why not?"

The question stabbed into Gavin with the sharpness of a scalpel. He didn't reply. How could he confess that the thought of facing Christa was more than he could handle? Did his inner struggle show in his face? Perhaps, for the doctor — who was known more for his medical skill than his bedside manner — grunted.

"I can send you to a military convalescent

center for a time, if you like."

"Thanks." Gavin's sense of relief was out of proportion to the simple offer. When he was alone, he fell into a deep sleep, the best he'd had since awakening to discover his career had been shot down.

Gavin continued to be troubled by the feeling that there was something urgent he had to do. Until he could settle things in his own mind, he didn't want to see Christa. "Wrong," he muttered. "I do want to see her. I want her here in my arms. I want to hear nothing has changed, and that as soon as I get back to Anchorage, we'll be married."

At that moment, Gavin Scott entered his own Garden of Gethsemane. He raised a mental wall to shut out the image of the woman he loved floating down the aisle of the church back home. The desire to ignore his qualms and go ahead with the wedding — as he and Christa had planned so long ago — left great drops of sweat on his forehead. In the end, he overcame temptation. He obtained pen and paper and began a task even harder than staggering through the desert in order to reach a safe place.

CHAPTER 6

Alaska

The high beams on Christa Jensen Bishop's Ford Explorer cut through the darkness like twin sabers. For the past few weeks, night had sneaked up and enveloped the land earlier each evening. Christa didn't mind. Warm and snug with Aurora for company, she actually enjoyed the dying end of day. She watched a lopsided moon peer over the top of a nearby mountain, accompanied by a lady-in-waiting star. What a gorgeous night! How many more such autumn evenings would there be before winter gobbled up even more daylight?

Christa's growling stomach reminded her of how long it had been since she'd eaten. "Wonder what Susan will have ready for us when we get home?" she asked Aurora. Her furry companion's ears perked up and Christa laughed. "I'm glad Susan and I have a standing rule: Whoever gets home first starts supper."

Home. The same thrill Christa experienced each time she reached the "fairy-tale cottage" ran through her. Its lighted windows never failed to awaken a matching glow in her heart. Every time she stepped through the door, she paused and gave thanks to God for allowing Susan and her to live there. Christa always felt the cottage held out welcoming arms to those who entered. Of course, much of the house's appeal came from the Hagensons' carefully chosen decor. The "home sitters," as Susan facetiously dubbed herself and her sister, had fallen in love with the place as it was. They put out photos of Don and Leigh Bishop and other cherished bits and pieces but left everything else the same, subscribing to the "if it ain't broke, don't fix it" theory.

Christa pressed down on the accelerator. She had always loved coming home at the end of a busy day. Yet the challenges she now faced made time spent with Susan — and dreaming of the future — special. They often ate supper off trays in front of the living room fireplace. It had become the center of their home. Crackling flames highlighted the polished wood floors. They cast shadows on the natural wood paneling and intensified the colors in the woven Indian blankets on couch and love seat. They also enriched the carpeted staircase leading to the two tastefully furnished upstairs bedrooms, each with a small but perfectly appointed bath.

"We were strangers in a strange land," Christa mused. A laugh spilled out and Aurora perked up her ears. "Not for long, Lord. Between having the Hunters for neighbors and meeting a certain Major Scott, we didn't have time to be homesick!"

An image of her fiancé's smiling face danced in her mind. Where was he right now? What was he doing? When would he get enough leave for a quick visit home? They'd had far too little time together before duty called Gavin overseas. Much of the time, she didn't have a clue where he was.

Christa sighed and Aurora woofed. "I know. You miss him, too," she told her dog. "Phone calls and e-mail help, but it's still hard. Well, as the saying goes, 'This too shall pass.' " She dropped one hand to the malamute's thick fur. "Too bad the rest of the quote isn't, 'and the sooner the better!' Wonder if I'll have a message when I get home?"

Anticipation spilled into the timeless words of Thomas Chisholm's song "Great

Is Thy Faithfulness." How she loved the tribute to the steadfastness and provision of God! Now, as Christa sang one of the world's most beloved hymns, her heart filled with gratefulness. How well she understood the things Chisholm loved! Summer, winter, springtime, harvest. Sun, moon, stars. Peace. Pardon for sin. Strength for whatever each day might bring and an abiding hope for all the tomorrows. All were precious gifts God gave to His children.

The lights of Anchorage appeared and grew brighter. The moon reflecting on the snowcapped peaks and Cook Inlet reminded Christa of the night she had promised to marry Gavin. A wave of love and longing swept through her. Was any woman ever more blessed than she? "Thank You, Lord," she whispered. A moment later she added, "I just pray that someday you'll send Susan a man as wonderful as Gavin — if there is one!"

Smiling at her prejudiced point of view, Christa swung into the driveway next to the cottage. As expected, light streamed from the shining windows, bidding her come in and rest. Too hungry to unpack the Explorer, she got out, summoned Aurora, and hurried up the stepping-stone walkway. "Stop pushing," she told her dog, who had nearly crowded her off the porch. "You're no hungrier than I am."

She stepped inside. "I'm home. So is Aurora. You won't believe what happened to me today." She shrugged out of her parka and hung it on a peg by the door.

Susan popped out of the kitchen like a clown from a jack-in-the-box. Light from the kitchen streamed after her, turning her hair to spun gold. The aroma of good cooking followed. "Can't it wait until we dish up? I made spaghetti pie and salad and baked apples. I'm starving."

"So am I, but this is too good to keep to myself. It's the funniest thing that's happened to me since I got here. Don't you want to hear it?" A giggle escaped, followed by another.

Susan looked toward heaven as if pleading for patience. "Go ahead and tell me before you explode."

"I drove a hundred miles each way today, some of it on rough roads, to check out a woman who called in saying her husband had developed a mysterious rash. He was feeling 'too poorly' to drive. Besides, the truck was 'broke down,' but she 'allowed as how' someone had better look at her man. All the way there, I hoped and prayed it wouldn't be something contagious." Christa grimaced. "That family has more children than the old woman who lived in a shoe."

"So what happened?"

"I got lost twice but finally found the place." Christa felt mirth bubbling up inside her but kept a straight face. "Sure enough, the man was itching and scratching like crazy."

"Well?" Susan planted her hands on her hips. "What was it?"

Christa couldn't hold laughter in even one more minute. "Long johns."

Susan's mouth dropped open. "Long John's what? Is that some kind of disease native to Alaska? I've never heard of it. What did you do?"

Christa doubled over and laughed until tears came. "I gave him some ointment to help stop the itching and ordered him to either replace his wool underwear with cotton or at least wear something cotton next to his skin." She wiped her streaming eyes with the back of her hand. "Case closed."

Susan almost cracked up. "Why don't we write a story called *Long John's Complaint*? We could print a pamphlet, sell it to tourists, and make a fortune. Now if you can stop laughing, go get washed up and we'll eat."

"Gladly. Will you put Aurora out and feed

her, please?" She started upstairs.

"Sure." Susan opened the front door and pushed Aurora onto the porch. Her scolding voice floated up the stairs. "You're a malamute, not a lapdog. Remember?"

Christa heard Aurora's reproachful bark and grinned. When Mac and Jean Scott had discovered Aurora was allowed inside, they immediately told the Bishop sisters to correct the situation. Malamutes didn't sleep in houses. Period. That's why God created them with such heavy fur. However, the damage had already been done. Aurora obviously felt she deserved preferential treatment. The nightly routine of convincing her otherwise always ended with a disapproving stare and that same reproachful bark.

Susan's supper was delicious and left Christa content enough to purr. The "Shoe" family, as Susan persisted in calling them, had invited Christa to eat with them, but she suspected there was barely enough food to go around without her partaking. She made a mental note to report the need. She hoped the family wouldn't be too proud to accept help. Alaskans were an independent lot, for the most part. It often took the patience of Job and the wisdom of Solomon to make patients see that the social services available were not handouts but were funded in large part by taxes. When put that way, most reluctantly agreed to accept at least temporary help. The other way was to point out that the sooner family members were better nourished, the sooner they would have the energy to fend for themselves.

Christa sighed. The scope of her nurse-practitioner duties was wider than the treeless tundra. It involved dealing with every aspect of human need: physical, mental, emotional, and spiritual. It required caring and sympathy, plus the stability to cope with human suffering, emergencies, and other stresses. She had to be able to communicate with a wide variety of people, obtain medical histories, perform physical examinations, and diagnose and treat acute health problems — including injuries and infections. In addition, she must order, perform, and interpret lab work and X rays. Eight-hour days were rare.

"Yet there's nothing I'd rather do," she confessed to Susan when they settled down in front of the fire. "By the way, thanks for doing the dishes." She yawned. "You didn't have to, since you cooked."

"You needed to unpack your gear," Susan reminded. "One thing about my job is that

I don't have to bring it home with me."

"Really. What about all those patients you encounter at the VA?"

Her sister's eyes darkened, a sure sign Christa was on target. "About those . . ."

The ring of the doorbell, followed by Aurora's sharp bark from the porch, drowned out the rest of the sentence. Susan got up from her seat on the couch and crossed into the hall. "Are we expecting company?"

"Not that I know about." Christa stood and followed Susan. "Who's there?" she called, wondering why she felt apprehensive.

"It's Molly. Shush, Aurora. If you don't know me by now, you never will."

Susan opened the door. "Come in. We're 'home and peaceful,' as Dad says."

Their robust, pleasant-faced neighbor shook her head. "Thanks, but no. Richard and I just got home from taking a friend to the airport." She held a letter out to Christa. "This was mixed in with our mail. Your lights were still on, so I figured I'd bring it over. See you tomorrow." With a wave of her hand, she headed down the walk.

"Thank you," Christa called before glancing at the envelope. Her heart thumped, then slowly iced.

"Who's it from? Gavin?" Susan peered

over her sister's shoulder. "Great, but why is the return address a military convalescent center in Texas?"

Unaware of the cold night air rushing into the hall, Christa slit the envelope with her fingernail. A single page fell out. The same sense of foreboding that had troubled her when the doorbell rang returned, only now it was multiplied a hundred times.

"Don't stand there freezing," Susan ordered. She reached past Christa and closed the door. "Come back in the living room by the fire before we turn into icicles."

Christa silently obeyed, the unread letter clutched in white-knuckled hands. She stumbled to a chair, sank into it, and read:

Dear Christa,

I was on a reconnaissance mission and our engines caught fire. We punched out (ejected), but I was blinded. Surgery has restored my sight, but the Air Force has taken me off flight status permanently. This changes everything between us. I am staying in Texas for now. Please don't come. I need time to sort things out.

Gavin.

A postscript read:

Tell Dad and Mom not to worry and not to come to Texas.

The last six words were underlined in heavy black ink.

CHAPTER 7

Late October shivered into November. Autumn winds stripped deciduous trees of their golden leaves, leaving stark, bare branches to wave against the cobalt sky. Thanksgiving was just weeks away.

Christa's life felt as barren as the trees. How could she give thanks when Gavin's letters and continued insistence that she not come to Texas hovered in her mind? "If he loved me the way I thought he did, Gavin would want me with him," she told Susan after a particularly bad day. The solitude she once cherished while driving gave her too much time to think. Her mind went round and round like a chipmunk in a cage. Now she stared into the fire, watching hope die.

"It's because he loves you so much that he doesn't trust himself to see you," Susan softly said. "Gavin has been through a terrible ordeal. Give him time."

Her sister's wisdom cheered Christa. "All right." Hot tears stung the insides of her eyelids and tumbled out. "Waiting is so hard."

Susan sighed. "I know. Whoever first said, 'Men go off to fight; women wait' was right on target. Only now, women go off to fight, too." She closed her eyes and her face twisted. "Even those who stay home are engaged in war. You. Gavin's parents. Thousands of others who have loved ones engaged in trying to bring peace and justice to the world." Tears glistened in her long eyelashes. "Think of the army of military wives — and sometimes husbands — who are raising their children alone. They deserve medals, too. Medals for serving on the home front.

"This afternoon a World War II veteran dropped by my office. I'd met him once before. He talked about how his father fought in the First World War and how things haven't changed in over ninety years." She swiped at her eyes. "He said he thought I might like to see something. Then he handed me a piece of yellowed sheet music he said had belonged to his mother. I brought a photocopy home." She took the stairs two at a time and came back clutching a folded page. "We've heard the refrain, but listen to the rest of 'Keep the Home-Fires Burning.'

"They were summoned from the hillside,
They were called in from the glen,
And the Country found them ready
At the stirring call for men.
Let no tears add to their hardship
As the Soldiers pass along
And although your heart is breaking,
Make it sing this cheery song.

"Keep the home-fires burning
While your hearts are yearning,
Though our lads are far away
They dream of Home.
There's a silver lining
Through the dark cloud shining,
Turn the dark cloud inside out,
Till the boys come Home."

Susan's voice turned ragged. It took a long time for her to regain control and go on with the second stanza.

"Overseas there came a pleading,
'Help a Nation in distress!'
And we gave our glorious laddies.
Honor bade us do no less.
For no gallant Son of Freedom

To a tyrant's yoke should bend,
And a noble heart must answer
To the sacred call of 'Friend.' "

Only the crackle of the fire broke the silence that followed. Christa's heart ached. How well the stirring words, penned by Lena Guilbert Ford long ago, fit the turmoil of the twenty-first century! Suddenly Christa felt the burden of a world enmeshed in war. Nation against nation. Truth against the forces of evil, whose goal was to stamp out good — and God. Was this what Jesus had experienced — as recorded in Matthew 23:37 — when He stood on the hillside and cried, "O Jerusalem, Jerusalem, thou that killest the prophets, and stonest them which are sent unto thee, how often would I have gathered thy children together, even as a hen gathereth her chickens under her wings, and ye would not!"?

After a long time, Susan brokenly said, "There is a silver lining, Christa, behind every dark cloud. We just have to hang in there and wait until we find it." She hugged the photocopy of the song to her chest, crossed the room, and went up the stairs — leaving Christa strangely comforted.

A week later, Gavin came home.

■ ■ ■ ■

He hadn't wanted to return. Against his nature, he'd malingered until the Texas powers that be threatened to throw him out. "We need this space for those with problems far more serious than yours," his doctor bluntly told him. "Major Scott, the Air Force needs you. You can't fly for the military, but you can serve in other ways. Forget the past and get on with your future. But first, go home and whip yourself into shape. You're no good to anyone the way you are now." He paused. "You should be thanking God you're alive."

The physician's no-nonsense evaluation stung Gavin, but it also injected a gleam of light into his night-black mood. He hopped a military plane the next day, wishing he were at the controls instead of traveling as a passenger. Yet the constant question, *Where were You when I needed You, God?* never left him. Neither did the obsession that Christa might pity him. All the way to Anchorage, Gavin dreaded what he might see in the blue eyes that had formerly shone with love and trust.

What he actually found shocked him. He hadn't dreamed Christa Jensen Bishop's eyes could flash with such scorn. Or that her first words when he reached his parents' home and she unexpectedly opened the door would be, "It's about time you came home where you belong, Gavin Scott!"

He felt his jaw drop, heard his mother gasp, and his father chuckle.

"Excuse me?" was the best response he could manage.

"You heard me. Why didn't you want me to come to Texas?"

Gavin found himself at a loss for words. "I needed time to —"

"Time to decide if I'm no better than a teenager with a crush on a pilot?"

It was so close to the truth, Gavin felt blood rush to his face. He tried to cover with a poor attempt at a joke. "Well, they say the fancy wrapper sells the goods."

Christa's eyes darkened until they resembled an Arctic night. "I fell in love with *you,* Gavin Scott," she blazed. "Not your uniform. Not your pilot's wings. Got that?"

Never one to cower from even the most direct attack, he was left without a defense — defeated by a woman stronger at that moment than he. The thought did what nothing else could have accomplished. It penetrated the stunned state in which he'd lived since realizing the end of his dream —

and caused a reaction so unexpected, he wondered if he might still be feeling the effects of his injuries.

He laughed.

The guffaw began at his toes and gathered force. It came out with the speed of a rocket and just as loud. A quick glance at his parents' startled faces only made him laugh harder, but when he turned back to Christa, his mirth died. Misery had replaced her anger. Her face crumpled and a sob escaped.

Gavin opened his arms, only dimly aware when his mother and father slipped away. "Christa, I am so sorry." He gently pulled her close to him. "It's just that . . ." His voice trailed off.

She sagged against him, her bravado gone. "I know. I really do." All the tears she had tried so hard to keep inside came in a torrent. She wrapped her arms around him and held him as if she would never let him go.

Gavin's homecoming remained bittersweet. Yet Christa's anger had made something clear: Her feelings for him had not changed. Gavin rested his chin on her shining golden brown hair. He forced himself to lay aside his disappointment and concerns for the future. Being encircled by Christa's strong arms — and her love — was enough for the moment. The future would take care of itself.

Thanksgiving passed in an abundance of turkey and pumpkin pie. December rushed in with thousands of decorative lights. And with trees and Santas and manger scenes. Although fighting continued around the world, carols of joy and the spirit of Christmas present shimmered in the winter air.

Not everyone's heart held peace on earth and goodwill toward men. In spite of Christa's unexpected greeting when Gavin returned home, doubts returned. Doubts about himself. About God, who could have changed things. Even about Christa. Restlessness drove him. Night after night, after he left Christa at the door of the fairy-tale cottage, he tramped the streets until tired enough to fall asleep. "Lord," he prayed, "why can't I just trust You and leave everything in Your hands? I'm sure not doing great on my own."

No answer came. No lifting of the gloom that surrounded him like a cloud-infested Arctic night.

"How can I celebrate the birth of Your Son when I'm feeling torn apart inside?" he demanded. A pang went through him. Christmas had always been special. For the sake of those he loved, he must somehow piece together the raveled edges of his life enough to get through the holiday season.

Two days later, an unexpected visitor arrived at the Scott home where Gavin was recuperating.

A series of sharp jabs on the doorbell brought him out of a daydream in which he was soaring high in an indigo sky and following the North Star. The rude return to reality irritated him, so he remained parked on the living room couch.

"Gavin, someone wants to see you," his mother called. An odd note in her voice made him wonder, but annoyance at being interrupted overrode his curiosity.

"I'm coming."

"You'd better be. I don't have time to stand here all day," someone retorted. The next instant, a grinning, red-haired Air Force captain strode into the room.

Surprise left Gavin speechless, but only for a few seconds. "Ben! What are you doing here?"

"You invited me, remember?" Ben looked innocent. "Fine thing. I travel thousands of miles and all he can say is, 'Ben, what are you doing here?' "

His parrotlike imitation of Gavin's voice

was perfect. It elicited a giggle from Jean Scott and a reluctant smile from Gavin. He leaped from the couch and pounded his friend's back. "Be serious, Burgess Benjamin."

"Knock off the name-calling. Mind if I sit down?" He sat and continued. "I'm here because I'm on leave until those torn ligaments are completely healed." He smirked. "I'm too valuable to the military for them to take chances."

"Yeah, yeah. So how long can you stay? Until after Christmas, I hope."

Ben cocked one eyebrow at Gavin's mother. "Sure, if I won't be an imposition."

Jean beamed at him. "Imposition? You're as welcome as spring. Now if you'll excuse me, I'll leave you two to visit." She started for the door, then turned back to the men. "Gavin, would you like me to call and invite Christa for supper?"

"Great idea. Ask Susan, too." He gave Ben a knowing look. "If she doesn't have a date, that is."

"She'd better not," Ben grumbled after Jean Scott vanished. "You aren't the only reason I came to Anchorage." Never one to beat around the bush, he added, "So, what are you doing hanging around home when you could be using your experience to serve our country?" He sobered. "The way the world is, we're all needed."

"That's for sure." Gavin stood and crossed to the window. Guilt for spending so much time and mental energy worrying about what he could no longer do, instead of focusing on what he might be able to do, swept through him. Before he could tell Ben that his question had slashed through Gavin's regret and self-pity, Mackenzie Scott came into the living room wearing a grin the size of a cruise ship. Gavin's heart-to-heart with Ben would have to wait.

One look at Susan Bishop, lovely in pale blue slacks and sweater, robbed Captain Sharp of his bantering. He greeted Christa, appealing in yellow, then eagerly turned back to Susan. At first she seemed rather distant, but by supper's end, she was obviously more comfortable with him.

Under cover of the table conversation, Gavin whispered to Christa, "Ben looks smitten, and Susan seems interested."

Christa slipped her hand into his under the tablecloth. Her face glowed. "More so than usual. It must be Ben's open face and the admiration in those honest brown eyes. I'm glad he came." She squeezed Gavin's hand.

"So am I." Someday he would tell her just how much, but not now. He still had a lot of things to sort out — and a lot of inner healing that must take place. Yet surrounded by love and friendship, the task before him no longer appeared hopeless.

CHAPTER 8

Gavin Scott had never been subject to mood swings. Yet as day followed winter day, he bounced between the heights of happiness and the depths of discouragement like a small plane trying to land on broken asphalt. Time spent with Christa offered solace. Watching Ben Sharp pursue Susan Bishop provided entertainment. Yet when Gavin thought of what he had lost, bitterness returned. In a few weeks Christmas would be over. What would the new year offer?

One afternoon, after he returned from a long and brooding walk, his mother met him at the door. "You have visitors," she said. A puzzled look crept into her face. "A family named Thorsett. The wife says they are here to fulfill a mission."

"A mission?" Sweat trickled down Gavin's neck in spite of the cold day. Had a fellow flier died and left him a bequest? *No, God,* he mentally argued. Then he realized that if that were the case, civilians wouldn't be delivering anything. That was followed by the ominous thought, *They would if personal effects had been given to them.* Dreading what might lie ahead, Gavin stepped into the living room. Relief shot through him. If the contents of the package lying near the hearth contained personal effects of a downed flier, the four strangers seated facing the blazing fire wouldn't be smiling.

"Major Scott? I'm Mark Thorsett. This is my wife, Natalie, and our daughters, Mollie and Amber." He motioned toward the attractive woman and two adorable girls who appeared to be perhaps six and eight.

Gavin held out his hand, noting the firmness of the man's grip. "Have we met?"

"No, but we have something in common." Natalie Thorsett's smile widened. "Mrs. Olivia Forester was my third-grade teacher — and much more. After my mother died, Mr. and Mrs. Forester took me in."

"She was my second-grade teacher," Gavin said. "I kept in touch with her for years. About a year ago, I received a letter from a law firm in Boise saying I had been identified as a 'conditional beneficiary' in Mrs. Forester's will — that I'd be contacted by their office when the conditions had been met." He laughed. "I have to confess I didn't give it much thought, except for feeling sorry she'd passed on. The life of an Air Force pilot doesn't leave much time for speculation."

"The law firm was Graves and Billings, wasn't it?" Natalie asked.

"Yes, but how do you know?"

A smile flitted across her face. "I'm the 'condition.' "

Gavin shook his head. "I don't understand."

She grew solemn. The two little girls edged closer to her, and she dropped an arm around each of them. "Neither did I. This time last year, I was living in Seattle and just this side of down-and-out. I faced eviction and had no idea where Mark was."

Gavin felt a lump form in his throat. The thought of the small girls living on the street touched his tender heart.

"One day I received a letter from a law firm — Graves and Billings. It said Mrs. Forester had left me something in her will." She smiled wryly. "For the first time in weeks, I felt a ray of hope. Anything valuable enough for my old teacher to consider her 'most priceless possession' must have monetary value." She stopped. "I was shocked when I signed the necessary documents and received my 'inheritance.' " She nodded at Mark, who opened the cardboard box the Thorsetts had brought. "This is it."

Gavin felt his jaw drop. This? Who would leave a still-beautiful but worn patchwork quilt to a former student? Had Mrs. Forester grown senile in her final days?

Mark spread the quilt over his wife's lap. The two little girls snuggled under it.

"Major Scott, this quilt is much more than it seems. There were days when I wrapped it around myself and my girls. It felt as if I were literally encircled by my Savior's warm arms. It has brought blessings to my life that I can't even describe. I don't know what blessings it will bring to you, but I'm sure you'll find out."

"To me!" Gavin shook his head. "I don't understand."

"The conditions of the bequest were that I was to keep the quilt for one year, then personally deliver it to someone whose name would be disclosed at the appropriate time. Ample funds to accomplish this would be furnished. I couldn't help wondering who, and why it was important for me to deliver the quilt in person! I still don't know. Anyway, here we are." Her laughter echoed from the walls of the quiet room. "Mr. Graves also sent me a letter I was to bring to you." She opened her purse and took out an envelope.

Gavin wonderingly tore off the corner and removed the contents.

I don't know when or where you will receive this, Gavin, but I somehow feel it will come when you most need it. When I was a young woman living in Texas, a raging fire just before Christmas took my ancestral home and everything I owned except for the family Bible. Insurance replaced "things," but I found it impossible to cope. How could I celebrate the Savior's birth when I had lost so much?

A few weeks later, I was quoted in a national magazine by a reporter doing a series on grief and faith. When asked how faith helped me deal with my loss, I replied, "One day at a time."

Soon afterward, a large package arrived. A Pennsylvania family named Fisher had read the series. They felt God wanted them to send me the patchwork quilt the first Mrs. Fisher had made during her last days on earth. It was a reminder to her husband of her love — and God's. The compassion and concern shown by these strangers filled me every time I touched the beautiful covering. It helped bring comfort and healing.

Now I am nearing the end of my earthly journey. I look forward to meeting the Master Quilter. May my most priceless earthly possession, though worn thin in places from years of hard service, be a reminder: God uses the broken, mismatched bits and pieces of our lives to create something beautiful and lasting, just as Darcy Fisher did long ago.

Affectionately,
Olivia Forester

The words blurred. Coming when he so desperately needed comfort seemed nothing short of a miracle. Gavin managed to thank the Thorsetts and see them out. Then he slumped into a chair and reached for the quilt. He unfolded it and spread it over his knees, idly tracing the tiny stitches and worn pieces of yarn that held it together. Just like the love of God, holding the jagged pieces of his life together until he could again become whole. A feeling of peace stole through him and he wondered, *How can the jagged pieces of fabric — many patched and patched again — make me feel everything is going to be all right?*

Gavin sank back into his chair, still holding his inheritance. He remembered lessons in life he had learned from the teacher who loved her students and challenged them to do their best. He still remembered her insisting life's problems were not as important as the way you handle them. "There's no disgrace in making mistakes and falling down," she said. "Just in giving up and lying there."

Gavin squirmed. What would Mrs. Forester think of him now, falling to pieces because of adversity?

A mental image rose before him: Hubbard Glacier in Yakutat Bay, one of Alaska's largest, most spectacular glaciers. When softened by warm sea air and eroded by seawater, tremendous chunks of ice broke loose — "calved" — from three-hundred-foot-high ice cliffs and crashed into the bay. Gavin had witnessed the spectacle from both ship and plane. Watching the forces of nature at work always brought a feeling of awe at their relentless fulfilling of God's design.

Hands still on the quilt, Gavin felt a great upheaval begin in the depths of his being. It worked upward, churning, building, like an avalanche gathering momentum. Helpless to stem the flow, he could only wait for it to end. It did not. Like a mighty flood that sweeps away whatever is in its path, Gavin's emotions raged in a final protest against the past, against the snatching away of his life's dream.

The feelings subsided. No voice whispered reassurance to his soul, but Major Gavin Scott had won a crucial battle against his worst enemy — himself.

Two years earlier, love had come to Christa and Gavin like a gentle breeze that blew into their hearts and became devotion. Now it attacked Susan and Ben like a March wind determined to sweep obstacles from its path.

Ben had come to Anchorage predisposed toward Susan because of Gavin's glowing description. One look into her aquamarine eyes convinced Ben she was as lovely inside as out. He prepared his strategy to win her as carefully as a general plans a campaign. His opening salvo was to privately tell Christa, "God willing, I plan to marry your sister."

"Good luck," she said. "Just don't think it will be easy." However, she had no answer to his reply that anything worth having was worth fighting for. She also was left speechless when one night shortly before Christmas, Susan ruefully confessed, "I feel as if

I've been caught up in a whirlwind." Susan stared into the blazing fire. "I never dreamed my 'Mr. Right' might turn out to have curly red hair."

"Are you serious?" Christa felt compelled to add, "If you marry Ben, it will mean lonely days and nights, raising your children as a single mother when he's away, and having your heart leap to your throat when he's overseas and you don't know where."

"I know. I saw what you went through when Gavin was gone." Susan shifted position in her chair and turned her poignant gaze toward Christa. "It doesn't matter. Don't get me wrong. I'm not going to run off and get married anytime soon." She blushed. "Even if I wanted to, Ben would never agree. He vowed after his parents' messy divorce that he'd never marry anyone unless he knew it was God's plan."

"And you think this may be?" Christa held her breath.

In a twinkling, Susan changed from serious to her usual pert self. "Did I say that?" Little sparkles danced in her eyes. "I don't think so." She sprang to her feet and planted her hands on her hips. "I'll tell you one thing, though. If Ben turns out to be Mr. Right, I'll follow him to the ends of the earth!"

Christa gaped, but Susan wasn't finished.

"Why did I ever think God sent the guy who dumped me?" She cringed, then fiercely added, "I've only known Ben a short time, but he has more integrity in his little finger than the jerk in Seattle has in his whole body."

"Hear, hear!" Christa began singing, "I'm in Love with a Wonderful Guy," but Susan only grinned and waltzed out of the room. Her going left emptiness. The thought of her marrying and leaving brought a pang. They had recently learned the Hagensons wanted to sell the fairy-tale cottage, but with Susan gone . . .

Christa shook her head. Who knew where Ben might be stationed? Or Gavin? She stirred uneasily. Although there had been great improvement in Gavin's attitude since he'd received the quilt, something she couldn't define still lay between them. On impulse, she picked up the phone and called him. "I know it's getting late, but Susan's gone to bed and I need to talk with you." Her heart raced like a jet plane during takeoff.

"What's on your mind?"

"Things don't seem right with us," she blurted out. The stillness that followed confirmed her suspicions. "Gavin, what's going on?"

When he finally spoke, he sounded despondent. "We're facing another hurdle."

Christa felt as if her heart had parked in her throat. "A–a hurdle?"

"Bigger than Mount McKinley. After a lot of prayer, I feel I'm supposed to stick with the Air Force, at least until this crazy world settles down. I don't know how they can use me, but I'm pretty sure I won't be stationed at Elmendorf." He hesitated so long, Christa's nerves screamed. "There's no guarantee there will be a need for a traveling nurse-practitioner where I'm stationed."

Relief sped through Christa like white water through a narrow gorge. "Is that all?"

"All!" His voice sharpened. "How will you feel if you have to give up the freedom of your present job for routine hospital work or private-duty nursing?"

Laughter bubbled out, along with a torrent of happy tears. "Even if it meant I could never practice nursing again — which it doesn't — it wouldn't matter. I can be happy anywhere, as long as we're together."

After a moment, Gavin huskily said, "I love you, Christa. More than life and second only to God Himself. Good night, my darling."

"Good night."

Long after they hung up, Christa curled up on the couch and searched her heart. Everything she had told Gavin was true, but she would miss Alaska. The fairy-tale cottage. Packing her Explorer and heading out to provide medical services to those who needed it, with Aurora in the "copilot" seat. Sadness filled her. How much chance was there of Gavin and her taking the malamute with them? Perhaps Gavin's parents would keep Aurora.

"Life is a trade-off," Christa murmured. "Part of my heart will forever remain in Alaska." She bowed her head. "God, Gavin and I know all things work together for good to those who love You, but right now it's hard to see how it applies to his being grounded. Please help us to trust You."

The fire slumbered and died. Her heart at peace without Christa fully understanding why, she deserted her post and went upstairs to a much-needed rest.

CHAPTER 9

Gavin Scott had always found submission difficult. Even though he'd long ago installed God in his life as his commanding officer, the words "Thy will be done" tended to stick in his throat. "After all," he reasoned, "God gave me a brain, so He must want me to use it."

Yet as Christmas and January rushed at him with the speed of sound, Gavin tired of trying to predict his future. The thought of a desk job appalled him. Pushing pencils was no career for a white hawk, even one that had been grounded. After a sleepless night, he got up, shrugged into warm clothes, and stepped outside, reveling in the frosty morning. He ran for miles. Each ground-covering step brought the growing conviction that he needed to stop trying to fight circumstances beyond his control. He reached a viewpoint overlooking the city just as the sun burst over the mountains, flooding the world with light that penetrated Gavin's self-sufficiency.

"You win, Lord. Whatever You have in mind will be okay with me." He waited, half expecting some kind of sign to show that God had heard and accepted his surrender. None came. The whitecaps on Cook Inlet continued unabated. The mountains behind Gavin didn't move an iota. He sighed and turned toward home and breakfast.

His mother met him at the door. "A Colonel Foster called."

Gavin's heart lurched. "What does he want?"

"You." She grinned. "His exact words were, 'Mrs. Mackenzie, tell that son of yours to get his b—' " She smiled again, her cheeks showing a modest blush, and then continued, " 'Begging your pardon, ma'am — get himself out here to Elmendorf immediately. I need him.' " Her eyes shone. "It sounds as if he has a job for you."

The words, *Hey, God, I really didn't expect an answer so soon,* flitted through Gavin's mind, then, *Too bad I didn't turn the controls over to You sooner.* He showered, shaved in record time, then crammed down a piece of toast to appease his growling stomach. Less than an hour later, he reached Elmendorf Air Force Base, manned by more than six thousand military personnel from all branches of the U.S. and Canadian armed forces.

Colonel Foster's abrupt opening words hit Gavin right between the eyes. "I need someone to command our survival-training program. You've had recent experience in escape and evasion. Not many can say that." His sharp gaze impaled Gavin and made him squirm.

"I was blind, sir. Captain Sharp is the one responsible for getting us to safety."

Colonel Foster snorted. "Doesn't matter. You understand what it feels like to go through such an experience. You've been there. Those you train will respect that. Besides, Captain Sharp's report attributed your survival to your leadership and especially your courage after being blinded. You also know Alaska. So, are you interested?"

Gavin had the insane urge to hug the brusque officer from sheer joy. "Yes, sir!"

"Good." The colonel permitted himself a wintry smile. "Report for duty January 2. Dismissed."

Gavin managed to salute and get back to his car without letting out a *yee-ha*. All the time he'd been wondering how even God could bring good out of his being grounded, this had been pending. Being trained in

214

survival skills made the difference between life and death. He, Major Gavin Scott, would be part of it — because of the accident. His new job also meant he would be based at Elmendorf. Christa could continue her nurse-practitioner work. At times, it might blend with his. And he would fly again — not Ravens hunting for enemies, but small Cessnas on search-and-rescue missions with the Civil Air Patrol.

"Thank You, God!" Gavin's mind raced ahead with rosy plans. He and Christa could begin planning their wedding. He would also look into buying the fairy-tale cottage. He grinned. If the way Susan and Ben looked at each other were an accurate indicator, Susan wouldn't be living there forever!

Winter melted into spring then early summer. With the dwindling snow and ice went the remnants of Gavin Scott's regret. He still felt a pang at seeing military aircraft soaring in the Alaskan skies. Yet the patchwork quilt served as a constant, loving reminder of the way God had picked up the ragged pieces of Gavin's life and had created from them a wholeness. Training men and women how to survive calamitous circumstances could result in saved lives.

John 15:13 often came to mind: "Greater love hath no man than this, that a man lay down his life for his friends."

"That's kind of what God has done with me," Gavin mused on his way to meet a new batch of trainees one morning. "I've had to lay aside what I believed was my life, in order for others to live."

While her fiancé settled into his new command, Christa continued her beloved nurse-practitioner duties. Aurora slept away many miles of their travel time. Christa — free from worry about the future — dreamed of the late autumn wedding when she would become "Mrs. Major."

The fairy-tale cottage would be a honeymoon cottage, for Susan had flatly announced, "You're not going to miss out on buying this place because of me." She tossed her blond head. "I have plans of my own." She refused to explain, but the frequency of letters from Captain Ben Sharp and the glow in Susan's face offered undeniable evidence of which way the wind was blowing.

An urgent call late one Sunday night changed everything. Susan hung up the phone, looking dazed. "Ben's been declared fit for duty," she told Christa. "He wants me to marry him next weekend." Excitement replaced shock. "Will you help me?"

Christa's heart thudded. After all their years together, the time for parting had come. She wasn't prepared, but she wouldn't spoil her sister's happy anticipation. "Of course. Will you call Dad and Mom, or do you want me to?"

Six days later, Susan Bishop became Burgess Benjamin Sharp's bride and began life as a military wife. Christa clung to her sister. "Be happy," she whispered.

Nothing could daunt Susan. "I intend to." She sent a loving look toward her new husband. "After all, I married 'Mr. Right.'" They drove away on a wave of laughter.

Summer made way for autumn. Gavin and Christa planned their wedding to coincide with Ben's leave. He and Susan arrived a few days beforehand, and the foursome planned a day of skiing. At the last minute, Christa felt she should check on an isolated patient before leaving on her honeymoon. Susan decided to go with her.

A wicked storm blew up out of nowhere. It caught Gavin and Ben on the slopes. A whiteout followed. Despite having taken precautions, their situation was precarious. Now was the time to use every bit of survival skill they possessed. As they began digging a snow cave, Ben wisecracked, "Talk about déjà vu. Only this time, we're definitely not in the Middle East!"

Gavin grunted. "You can say that again. On the other hand, I can't see any better now than I did then! I just hope Christa and Susan are okay and not out on some back road."

"God can take care of them," Ben reminded. "But it doesn't keep me from wishing we were with them." He continued digging. "All we can do is hunker down and wait."

Miles away, Christa repeated the words. "All we can do is wait. At least we're safe and snug in a winter-proofed home." She smiled at her patient — who was doing fine and was obviously delighted to have the sisters snowed in with her — and looked directly at Susan. "Don't worry about the guys. Both are skilled in the art of survival."

"Yes, but there's a whole lot more snow in the mountains than here. I intend to keep up a barrage of prayers," Susan declared.

"Good idea. In the meantime, we wait."

It wasn't easy. Even knowing no one was better equipped to face a winter storm than Gavin and Ben didn't melt the nagging uncertainty of wondering how their men were faring. It took all of Christa's faith and Susan's "barrage of prayers" to make it through the seemingly endless day, then the next.

On the second morning after the storm, an apologetic sun came out. So did Gavin and Ben, crawling from their shelter like bears after hibernation. They wasted no time in getting off the mountain.

Christa, Susan, and Aurora just as quickly made an exit of their own. They actually made it back to Anchorage a few tense hours before the men returned.

As if to make up for its unexpected assault, the weather stayed beautiful. Two nights later, a curious moon peered down on the church where Gavin and Christa first met — the church where they now took their vows. Gavin looked deep into Christa's blue eyes, humbled by the love shining brighter than the brightest star in the heavens — a God-given love that Gavin knew would never die.

The "white hawk" had never soared higher.

EPILOGUE

Just before Thanksgiving, Gavin Scott received a letter from the law firm of Graves and Billings, Attorneys-at-Law. The names didn't immediately register. "Do they think I'm going to sue the Air Force?" he grumbled.

Christa laughed. "Hardly. Isn't Graves the name of Mrs. Forester's attorney?"

"Right." Gavin tipped open the envelope and pulled out the single page. "Listen to this:

'To Amy Fisher Nelson, Natalie Thorsett, and Gavin Scott. Mrs. Olivia Howard Forester left a final request. You and your families are to gather at Sun Valley the weekend before Christmas to share the full story concerning the patchwork quilt. You will also decide who is to keep it. All expenses will be paid.' "

Gavin looked at his wide-eyed bride. "Sun Valley? Start packing!"

The weekend before Christmas, the Scotts, Thorsetts, and Amy Nelson and her husband, Tim, eagerly joined Mr. Graves in the large firelit meeting room he had reserved. Amber Thorsett tugged on Natalie's sleeve and pointed to Amy, who sat holding the worn heirloom quilt. "Look, Mom. She's holding our quilt. Do you think she's the one who made it?"

Her mom smiled. "I don't think so, honey, but maybe she knows something about the person who did make it."

"Do you think she'll tell us?" Natalie's other daughter, Mollie, asked.

Before Natalie could reply, Amy nodded her curly, dark head and obligingly began. "Once upon a time, more than sixty years ago, a beautiful lady named Darcy Fisher lived in Easton, Pennsylvania. Just before she went to heaven, she made a quilt for her husband, Dan. Working on it brought great comfort to her. Dan Fisher hung his wife's gift in their used-toy shop, Twice Loved." Amy's eyes grew misty. "My father was killed in World War II, but when I was six, Mama and I met Dan. He and my mother later married. I loved my new daddy, and I loved to cuddle up in the quilt he gave me for Christmas that year."

"So did we," Amber said. "We didn't have anyplace to live, but Mommy and Mollie and I would wrap the quilt around us, and we always felt warm. Our daddy says it protected us when his arms weren't there to protect us. I loved the quilt. Mollie and I wanted to keep it, but Mom told us it was just ours for a year. Dad said now that he was with us and could keep us warm and safe, God knew someone else needed it more."

Amber turned to Gavin. "Did it make you happy?"

Gavin smiled at her earnest face. "Very happy."

Amy went on. "When we read an article about Olivia Howard, who had lost everything except her Bible in a terrible fire, we decided to send her the quilt to make her feel better. Our families became friends. Olivia and her new husband, Nate Forester, came to Pennsylvania and later moved to Boise. I can't help thinking how happy Darcy would be to know all the stories about her quilt."

Natalie looked puzzled. "I still don't understand why Olivia Forester chose Gavin and me to inherit it."

Mr. Graves held up his hand like a school-boy. "My turn. A few years ago, Olivia insisted I draw up a new will for her. She said God wanted her to do so. You don't argue with that kind of reasoning!" Laughter rippled around the room, and Mr. Graves continued, "Olivia loved Christmas. She loved hearing from her former students, but that year she was saddened by the pain and loneliness that showed beneath the cheery holiday greetings. How could she, with limited resources, help? Besides, she sensed what many of her former students really needed was love, friendship, and to know God.

"Olivia decided she could at least help a few and asked God to help her choose. Gavin, she laughed and laughed at your postscript." He quoted, " 'I've been so busy, I haven't had time to find a woman with whom to share my life. God willing, some-day I will.' Feeling all was well with you, she tossed the card aside."

"That was the last Christmas before I met Christa," Gavin interjected.

"One card offered no news," Mr. Graves said. "Just the signature: 'Natalie.' Olivia recognized the writing. She assumed Nat-alie wasn't married or she'd have signed her full name. In Olivia's own words, 'At that moment a matchmaker was born.' Gavin and Natalie were fairly close in age. What if she made it possible for them to meet?"

Gavin felt like he'd just been dunked in a glacier-fed lake. "What if she *what?*"

Natalie gasped. "So that's why I had to deliver the quilt to Major Scott in person!"

"Keep in mind, Olivia felt she was doing God's will," Mr. Graves told them.

"What a schemer!" Despite his annoyance at his teacher's outlandish scheme, Gavin couldn't help laughing. "God has some sense of humor! He used Mrs. Forester's matchmaking attempts to get the quilt to Natalie when she needed it — and then to me."

"How could Olivia perceive needs that hadn't yet arisen?" Christa wondered out loud. "All she had to work with were a loving heart, a Christmas card signed 'Natalie,' and a hastily scrawled postscript."

"Olivia only thought she knew," Amy quietly put in. "It was God who really knew."

Mr. Graves looked from face to face. "For six decades, the old quilt has been a comfort and a joy. Now you must decide who will be its keeper. There's one provision: If someone is ever found with a greater need for the quilt, the keeper must pass it on."

Gavin glanced at Amy. Her eyes were soft with memories. Surely she deserved the inheritance. Yet Natalie had suffered. As for him, parting with the patchwork quilt would be like losing a dear friend.

Amy soberly said, "We could split the quilt in three pieces, but that's not what Mrs. Forester requested. I vote for Gavin."

Natalie chuckled. "So do I. It will give our family an excuse to go to Alaska again!"

Gavin wordlessly accepted the heirloom. He draped it over his arm and walked away with Christa, too moved to speak.

One by one, the others said good night and went to their rooms, leaving Mr. Graves to stare into the dwindling flames. He thought of a passage of scripture — Luke 2:10–12 — which referred to the long-ago night when Hope had come to earth; a night when angels announced the birth of Jesus to a group of humble shepherds in the fields near Bethlehem: "Fear not: for, behold, I bring you good tidings of great joy, which shall be to all people. For unto you is born this day in the city of David a Saviour, which is Christ the Lord. And this shall be a sign unto you; Ye shall find the babe wrapped in swaddling clothes, lying in a manger."

When the last ember flickered and died,

Mr. Graves spoke to his Master. "Lord, I have carried out my task. Olivia's dream has been fulfilled. Peace and friendship surround those who gathered here because of her. Surely these blessings will continue to warm them all, just like the patchwork quilt and the swaddling clothes that once wrapped Your gift to the world."

Then, deep within the faithful servant's heart, a voice whispered in tones so hushed yet clear that Mr. Graves felt as if he were on holy ground. *"Yes, My son, for both the quilt and the swaddling clothes were created in love and bestowed with great joy."*

ABOUT THE AUTHOR

Colleen Reece learned to read beneath the rays of a kerosene lamp. The kitchen, dining room, and her bedroom in her home near the small logging town of Darrington, Washington, were once a one-room schoolhouse where her mother taught all eight grades!

An abundance of love for God and each other outweighed the lack of electricty or running water and provided the basis for many of Colleen's 140 books. Her rigid "refuse to compromise" stance has helped sell more than 4.5 million copies that help spread the good news of repentance, forgiveness, and salvation through Christ.

The employees of Thorndike Press hope you have enjoyed this Large Print book. All our Thorndike, Wheeler, and Kennebec Large Print titles are designed for easy reading, and all our books are made to last. Other Thorndike Press Large Print books are available at your library, through selected bookstores, or directly from us.

For information about titles, please call:
(800) 223-1244

or visit our Web site at:
http://gale.cengage.com/thorndike

To share your comments, please write:
Publisher
Thorndike Press
295 Kennedy Memorial Drive
Waterville, ME 04901